Dancing In the Rain

The final cut

Dancing In the Rain

The final cut

- Based on a True Story -

Tara L. Nicole

PNEUMA SPRINGS PUBLISHING UK

First Published 2006
Published by Pneuma Springs Publishing

Dancing in the Rain: The Final Cut

ISBN10: 1-905809-02-6
ISBN13: 978-1-905809-02-8

Cover design, editing and typesetting by:
Pneuma Springs Publishing

A Subsidiary of Pneuma Springs Ltd.
230 Lower Road, Belvedere Kent, DA17 6DE.
E: admin@pneumasprings.co.uk
W: www.pneumasprings.co.uk

A catalogue record for this book is available from the British Library.

To *A. Tianna: who has been there through it all; supporting me, loving me, and teaching me to laugh time and time again. To you I owe my life, so many times over.*

To my sister: who never stopped believing in me, or this book, when even I was ready to give up.

And to Tom, Jared, and Dara: at 21 I have had the privilege of falling in love three times and there is no greater gift than that. So thank you, you will always have a piece of my heart.

AUTHOR'S NOTE:

"What is your book about?" People ask when they hear my book got published. And I always pause, and have to think about that for a moment. "It's a coming of age novel" I answer at last. It is about growing up, about finding yourself. It is about first loves, and the crushing power of letting go of those you love. It is about finding the strength within yourself, and knowing that only you have the power to save yourself. But it is also about depression and self-mutilation.

Self mutilation has sometimes been quoted as the "new anorexia" with a reported 2 million cases in the US alone. It is estimated that one out of every 200 teen girls between the ages of 13 and 19 regularly practise self-harming behaviour*. These numbers are staggering. By the time I was sixteen, some disorder be it cutting, burning, safety pins, depression, anorexia, bulimia, or suicide, were all just part of life. Despite its common occurrence, each one of us feels alone, as if we are the only one going through this hard time.

My hope for this book is to remind those who feel they are alone that they are not. You are never truly alone, no matter how much you think no one cares, someone does. So reach out: to a parent, a friend, a school councillor, or a help line. It doesn't matter who, just make sure it is someone who will act accordingly. And to everyone else: sixteen doesn't make you an adult, it doesn't mean you can conquer the world, we are never really as strong as we appear.

This, however, is my story; just one in a thousand. It is not how it is for everyone. It is not even exactly how it was for me. It is just how it felt. The people in this book have been altered, combined, dramatized, the events invented, manipulated or twisted by my perception of the world. So anyone who knows me may find a piece of themselves in this book, and to them I say, thank you. No matter what your role was; to push me to my lows or drag me out of them, you have shaped me, and for this I am grateful. I am truly blessed in my life for having gone through all I have I will always appreciate life that much more. And no matter how much each heartbreak hurts I will continue to love: fully, foolishly, and completely because I have faith that one day, I will get my happily-ever-after ending. In the end hope will always win out and I would encourage everyone, at least once, to go dancing in the rain because, well, it's always worth it and there is always something worth celebrating.

Tara L. Nicole

Comments? Questions? Or for more information on Self-harm please feel free to email me at: TaraLNicole@gmail.com

* 2002 Essortment.com

Everything is okay in the end,
if it's not okay, then it's not the end. – Anonymous.

PRELUDE

PRESENT DAY: DRUE'S 22nd BIRTHDAY

I look around. The restaurant is not crowded, but there is a scattering of people through out the small room: a couple sit in the corner entirely involved in each other, a group of young girls giggle and laugh together, a husband and wife sit each with their own section of the newspaper comfortable in silence, a mother sits at the counter with her young daughter who turns about on the stool unable to remain still, a man further down reads the paper. I sit by the window. The warmth from the restaurant has left a slippery layer of condensation on the glass. I trace my finger through it, following the line of trees just outside. People rush by on their way to work, completely oblivious of the small restaurant on the corner.

The waitress comes over. She is of an age that I now consider young, though she would never say the same about herself. She has blond hair thrown into a messy bun on the top of her head and her dark eye make-up gives the impression that she has not slept well in days. I order. She raises her eyebrows. "It's for two," I explain.

"Ya got company comin'?"" she asks between chews of her gum, sounding skeptical that "my company" will ever arrive.

I nod. "She will be here any minute." Just then I see her. She is still two blocks away, but clearly visible as she nimbly weaves her way between the oncoming traffic. Her bohemian skirt dances around her legs, her sunglasses balance precariously on top of her head. She holds her high-heeled shoes in hand, running without putting heel to pavement as if striving to at least protect this portion of her foot from the dirty street. She hurries along unaware of the strange sight she creates. Her hair is in a loose ponytail at her neck, a piece escapes and falls in her eye forcing her to reach up and brush the offending hair aside in an action that she performs subconsciously in rhythm with her steps. As she approaches the restaurant she stops and drops her shoes to the ground where she slides her feet into them. She smoothes her skirt, pushes her bag further up on her shoulder, brushes her hair behind her ear and then opens the door. I stand as she enters and give a small wave. Drue smiles and comes over.

"I am so sorry," she begins before she reaches me, "I had to park like miles away, damn tourists," she adds with a smile.

I return the smile, and give her a hug. "Happy Birthday."

She rolls her eyes, "22. Woo-hoo."

"Yeah well they can't all be 21," I respond.

She slides into the seat across from me with a sigh, "yeah that was a good one, wasn't it?"

I laugh. "For you, no doubt it was."

She clicks her teeth grinning. "So did you order?"

"Yeah."

"You are the best."

I just smile. Our waitress approaches, placing the orange juice and coffee in front of me then stares blankly at Drue daring her to order again.

"Coff-" Drue begins, then I slide the coffee that was just set down towards her, she looks at me and grins. "I was going to be surprised if you had taken up the habit." She looks to the waitress. "Never mind." The waitress just looks back blankly then walks away.

"Well she's not very nice," Drue comments.

I shrug, "it's early."

"Yeah it is. You and your stupid work schedule."

"Hey it's still an improvement from High School."

"God yeah, what time were those breakfasts, quarter to six or something? We were insane. How were we ever that dedicated?"

"We never actually studied anyway, all a bit pointless."

"Yeah…" She is silent for a minute, turning her coffee cup slowly. "Feels like forever ago," she says at last. "Wouldn't it be fun to meet ourselves freshman year, to go back and see who we were then?"

I raise my eyebrows. "I was so weird. Why were you ever my friend?"

Drue shrugs. "I couldn't get rid of you." She grins.

I laugh. "Thanks."

"Hey, we are still friends. See, so you came around?" She takes a sip of coffee then begins again, "so how is life?"

I shrug, "same old. You know this town."

She looks out the window. "Yeah, some things really never change do they? Same beautiful town, full of beautiful people. Feels more phoney every time I come back." We both look out of the window, watching the people as they pass our window - in suits late for the office, with strollers taking their kids for a walk, loaded with bags already weighed down from a day of shopping, or in track suits for an early morning run. All of them in the latest fashions, hair perfectly in place, clean shaven, make-up perfectly applied, no one more than five pounds over weight, and even now in the dead of winter, no one without a respectable layer of tan. It really is perfect. Drue shakes her head. "At least the weather is nice, was getting so tired of snow Back East, nice to have the sun."

I nod in agreement then change the subject. "Any new boys?"

Her smile broadens. "Jealous are you?" She teases, then shakes her head. "No one important. And you? Any girls I have to go beat up?"

"Drue, honestly."

She shrugs. "Just checking."

We sit in silence for a moment. She takes her coffee in both hands gathering warmth from the mug.

Our waitress returns with our food. "Fruit and granola?"

Drue smiles. "Ohhh good choice. I mean, that's for me thanks."

The waitress is not amused. She puts the plate of food in front of us. I pass my tomatoes to Drue. "Thanks," she says taking them from me happily.

"No problem."

"So?" Drue raises her eyebrows at me. "What's new?"

The question is innocent enough; it is how Drue always begins our conversations. It is then my job to pick the direction. However, I pause for a moment before answering. Might as well get right to it, I decide. "I want to write a book about you." I tell her.

Drue blinks and her eyes go wide. She sets her cup on the table. "You are that bored?"

I laugh. "No."

"Then why would you want to write about me? I've led a pretty standard life Chris."

"You have a story to tell. I want to tell it," I say simply.

"But…. why?" Her forehead furrows and I can't tell if she is angry or only confused.

I sigh, how can I explain? How can I tell Drue that her story is one that must be told, not because it is unique or complex, but because it is the story of so many young girls. It is the story of love, of loss, of pain, of healing and most of all, of strength. How can I explain this to Drue, who sees her story only as proof of her weakness? I just smile. "Ah, I ran out of material, and figure I now have to start taking the stories off my friends for inspiration."

"But for real? You are really going to write a book?"

I nod.

"That's cool, I guess."

"So it's okay? You'll let me interview you?" I sit watching my friend process this idea. I know what I am asking of Drue, how hard it will be to drag up all the old memories that she has worked so hard to forget, to move on from, to let go of, and the only thing I don't know is what it will take out of her. However, with true 'authoretic' passion I think only of the desired end, hoping as I do, that I don't destroy my best friend in the process.

At last she sighs, "I'm a damn good friend."

I smile. "This I already know. I need to know everything else."

"Alright, where do we begin?"

I get out my pen ….

FRESHMAN YEAR: The Beginning

"We do not remember days, we remember moments" - Cesare Povese

PRESENT DAY: TWO WEEKS LATER

I stare at my computer screen. It is blank. It has been blank, in fact, for the past three hours. Complete and utter writer's block. I sigh.

There is a knock at the door.

"Come in," I say grateful for the distraction.

"Hey." The voice is one so completely familiar; it takes me a moment to realize how out of place it is in the current setting.

I look up at my visitor and smile. "Hey, I thought you were leaving today?"

She smiles. "I am. Two hours. I just wanted to stop by and give you these." She holds out a stack of books to me. They are an odd assortment of different sizes, shapes, colours and patterns. I set them on the table.

"Can I get you anything? A drink?"

She smiles and shakes her head; her hair is black for winter, and now in its straightened state hangs down to the middle of her back. She tucks it back behind her ear, more out of habit than necessity. "Nah I'm good. I can't stay long anyway. My mom will start to worry if I cut it too close."

"Yeah of course," I respond.

She comes over and puts her hands on the back of my chair looking at the computer screen in front of me. "How's it coming?"

I don't say a word, just gesture in way of the blank screen. She nods, "that good huh?"

"So what are these?" I ask, searching for a change in topic. I pull the books towards me, taking the one off the top and inspecting the cover. It is a small book, with a pink cover and a gold trim along the edges of its pages. It once had a lock, but has been opened and closed so many times that it is now rendered useless, hanging to one side rather than being snapped together as it was intended to. I open to the first page and instantly recognize Drue's looping handwriting.

"My journals." She explains. "They should help, I think. Probably more than me anyway."

I look up at her with surprise. "Are you sure?"

"Yeah. Read 'em. See what you can learn. They probably aren't all true, but they are at least how I saw the world."

I stare at the page in front of me. Drue's childish handwriting holding all the secrets of her fifteen year old self. "Thank you." I finally say.

"No problem." She turns to leave. When she gets to the door, she pauses, looks back. She purses her lips, one side of her face going up in a smile, she gives a small nod. "Good luck," she says at last.

"Thanks. I'll talk to you soon?"

"Yeah, I'll be home again for Spring Break, if you want to get together then."

As the door closes behind her, I turn back to the book in front of me. Drue's diaries have been a part of her as long as I have known her, coming with her on every trip, always hidden in the depth of her bag at school. And yet they have always evaded my eyes. I would tease her at times, about reading them, or stealing them, and she would laugh and just say "maybe one day", but I never actually expected to be granted that privilege. Now, here they are sitting in front of me, holding, I hope, the solution to my current writer's block. Still, I am a bit nervous as I open that first page, my heart beat is just a bit faster than normal, and I wonder if I am ready to read the inner thoughts of a girl that I have known for seven and half years, and yet who has always remained a mystery to me. And so, with trembling hands, I settled back into my chair and begin to read.

Four hours later, I find myself ready to write.

1

August 30th

Dear _____

Hello! Welcome! I'm sorry you don't have a name; I just can't seem to think of the right one yet. You are to be my journal for my freshman year of High School. I'm going to be a freshman! How crazy is that? So old! And I just can't think of a suitable name. But it will come. Soon. I promise. Until then-

My name is Drue Elizabeth Potter. I am fourteen years old. I have one older sister, two parents, no dog, but otherwise our life is pretty storybook. I like it that way. I've never been much a fan of drama, that's Stacey's (my sister) specialty. I've never been in love. I've kissed a boy, once, on a dare, but that doesn't really count. Maybe this year that will all change. I hope so. I'm starting a new school. And I'm a bit nervous, I don't know anyone, well other than Stacey and she's two grades my senior. But I suppose it'll be an adventure. So, wish me luck! And welcome. This is my world.

Yours always, Drue Potter

The air smelled like honeysuckles. She would remember that smell for years to come. Honeysuckles mixed with freshly cut grass and the salt blowing in from the sea. The breeze rustled her hair and rocked the hammock softly beneath her. She could almost feel summer slipping away from her as she lay staring up at the leaves over head, they danced in the breeze, a slow, wistful dance of lovers. She liked their motion; it was not hurried or frantic, but lazy and relaxed as if they could dance like that forever. She smiled, wishing she could lie here forever, in the summer breeze just watching the leaves dance. She hummed to herself softly, not quite sure of the words to the song in her head, only that it was comforting, a song she had known her entire life. She closed her eyes and the leaves disappeared, but only for a moment, then they returned, dancing in the wind. She took a deep breath forcing herself to remember the smell along with the picture, promising herself she would never forget this last moment in the home that she loved so dearly. For the second time in her life, her family was moving away from this home to a new house that she neither knew nor loved. But she would go, and she knew in time, though it would never be the home this place was to her, she would grow accustomed to it, because, as they say, you can get use to anything.

She opened her eyes. She heard the truck pull into the driveway. The moment was gone. It was only a matter of time now before her mother noticed that Drue was not in the house packing up the last boxes as she had promised. Drue extracted herself from the hammock; all good things had to come to an end. She folded up the hammock, wondering as she did so if there would be a place for it in the new house. She carried it out to the driveway. Between the small cracks in the netting Drue could just make out her father standing beside the moving truck. "Oh good Drue, perfect timing. Here I'll take that. Is your room all done?"

"Yep, one more box."

"Great. Could you go get it please? We are running late and really need to get this last load over to the house."

Drue gave a small nod and walked back to the house.

Drue's mother was standing in the kitchen. Her hair, which had started the day pinned back in two small clips, had now mostly escaped, framing her face in a disarray of wisps and curls. She had cleaning gloves on and held a sponge in one hand, a broom in the other. She stared at Drue when she walked in. Drue tilted her head slightly wondering if her mother did in fact recognize her as her youngest daughter. "Drue, where have you been?"

"Out back, why? What's up?"

"Well I could have used some help here!"

Drue shrugged. "Why? You are doing fine. And Dad said it didn't need to be perfect anyway."

"He says that, but that just means we'll have to come back. Might as well get it all done today." She turned back to the floor, "I hate moving," she grumbled.

Drue sighed wondering how just a moment earlier the world had been in complete peace. Drue walked into her room. The room was small, she could cross the whole space in about five paces, something she had done continuously. This room had been created for her. When she was younger it had been the playroom, the place that had held all of her sister and her toys and magic, stories and games, all the things that made childhood something to be fantasized about. Then when they moved back and her sister begged for her own room, Drue had moved in here. Her father had created for Drue a window seat in the small bay windows, the only architectural design that Drue had ever cared about. It was here that Drue found herself now, running her hand along the cushion, a material that matched the pillow she had had made at the same time, a seat with which over the last two years she had spent the majority of her time on, reading, praying, crying, laughing, daydreaming. It was the place she had retired to when she had learned her great uncle had died, it was the seat that comforted her when Anne of Green Gables was all grown up and there were no more books to read, it was the seat where she made up her first staring roll in her fantasized movie, and it was the seat where she sat for hours in silence when her parents told her they were moving. No matter what the subject it always felt more romantic on that seat. Drue knew there would be no window seat at her new house. She looked out the window. The trees stared back at her blankly, daring her to cry, challenging her to survive without them. She just stared back.

"Drue! Drue where are you?"

"In here," Drue yelled answering her mother's call.

Her mother appeared in the doorway. "Dad is calling you. I thought you were all done? Why are there still boxes in here?"

"It's just one Mom. I'm about to get it."

"Well go now. Dad's closing up the truck."

"Okay." Drue got up from the seat. She picked up the box and walked outside.

The truck was closed. "Drue! I thought I told you to bring that right out. I just closed up the truck."

"Sorry?" Drue offered quietly. Drue left the box on the driveway and slid into the backseat of the car. Her sister was already there.

"Mom and Dad are a little tense."

Drue's sister looked at her sympathetically. "Yeah no kidding."

Drue smiled. She leaned her head against her sister and together they waited for her parents. Soon they were all in the car.

"Does everyone have everything?" Drue's dad turned around in his seat to stare down each girl in turn. "I don't want to have to come back. Everything is cleared out. Everyone double checked."

Each girl nodded in turn silently praying that it was in fact the truth- had she double checked the bathroom? What about the hallway closet? The car started and they pulled out of the driveway behind the moving van.

The family sat in silence oppressed by their own thoughts. Drue stared out the window, watching as her neighbourhood was replaced by new surroundings.

The drive didn't take long. The small California town that had been Drue's home for the entirety of her fourteen years was not large, the whole place could be driven through in about twenty minutes, which is what they were doing now: past stucco houses, the single mall downtown, the large stretch of palm lined beaches where all year round tourists came to surf, walk, bike and enjoy the sun. Then they came to her new neighbourhood. There were no oak trees here, no smell of salt in the air. Neighbours didn't walk their dogs down these streets, there were no kids riding bikes or selling lemonade along the sidewalk. Here there were only large houses, estates that held imposing gates to ward off uninvited guests. There were fancy cars with leather seats and vanity plates. Still, Drue could just make out palm trees in the distance and as they came over the hill to their new street, Drue could see the ocean. It was not the block walk her old house had been, but it would do.

The new house was smaller than its neighbours. It was the house I would come to know as well as I knew my own. The only house I would ever think of as hers. But she never did. It was never a true home for Drue. Not like that first house.

Drue walked into her new home and had the distinct impression she had walked into a mental institution. Not because it was particularly ugly, it was just so white. The carpets were white, the walls white, the blinds in the rooms were white and when you walked down the main hall to the bedrooms you could touch both white walls with your hands. Her old house had a green room to give the house character and an under the stair cranny to hide in. This house was just, white. Drue ran her hand along the walls as she walked, slightly afraid the walls would in fact close in around her if she was not careful. Her room was the second one down the hallway and when she walked in, she sighed. More white. The curtains, thick things that looked more stifling than welcoming, were the only colour in the room, providing a grey frame to the windows. A mattress lay on the floor for her, and her boxes lined the wall, she could just make out the white carpet in the cleared three feet of space by the door.

"Drue come look outside!" Her dad called from the backyard. Drue turned making her way down the small hallway and following through the last room on her right. She found her family standing just outside the glass doors staring at the backyard. "Look at the pool." Her dad was showing her mother and sister excitedly.

The pool was beautiful. It was oblong, with a small diving board at one end and a waterslide off to one side. In the cool August evening the water rippled invitingly.

"There is even a basket-ball court," her dad added, "admittedly it needs some work, but that can be fixed."

Drue smiled looking at what her dad was pointing at. It was a large concrete square beside the pool; the only reminiscent to a basketball court was the leaning hoop that stood at one end. "It's great Dad, really great," she said, trying to match her dad's enthusiasm. Then she turned and returned to her new room. Drue wasn't much in the mood for family time right now. She lay down on the mattress that was made up for her and stared at the blank ceiling.

This was to be her home for the next four years. After that she would be at college, and so whether her parents lived here, her old house, or a new one would have little bearing on Drue. She wondered what memories would be made in the walls of this house. What laughter would come from this room? What tears would be shed on this bed? Would she find what she had been searching for? She hoped that a new school and new people would help her find it. That person, thing or passion that would at last make her complete because as she lay there Drue was reminded of that empty feeling in her stomach; that hollowness that was waiting to be filled. It was going to be one hell of a year.

And with that, Drue rolled over, and closed her eyes.

She didn't know just what a year it would be. She couldn't have known then how her life was about to be changed forever. Not by me, though I wish it had been me rather than him that would take the title of the most influential person in her life. I would not have hurt her like he did. But then, I am getting ahead of myself, for as she lay there that night curled up on the floor, her black curls fanned out on her pillows, her forehead slightly furrowed from the anxieties of the day to come, Drue did not know either of us yet, all she knew was that a new school awaited her in the morning. The things that would come from the decision to break away from her friends and go to a new high school, those things were the workings of fate and still unknown to the sleeping girl as she dreamed that night.

2

September 4th

Dear Amor,

I have given you a name! It is in honor of my goal for this year. To find love. Not necessarily in a person, just to find a passion. Something to fill this void that has been in me since I can remember. I want to be whole. And the only thing I can think that will ever fill this is love of some kind or another. So that is your name.

Mom laughs at me because I talk to myself. But I also listen to myself. I also punish myself, and reward myself. I am proud of myself or embarrassed of myself. I get angry at myself or happy with myself. Aren't all those things normal? Why then is talking not? Oh yes, I forgot one thing of major importance. I comfort myself.

Night, Drue.

"God, that day was long." Drue sank into the passenger seat of the car and closed her eyes.

"Should I not ask how the day went?" Stacey said looking at her baby sister.

Drue opened her eyes. "Nah, it was fine. Just long. I thought classes would never end."

Her sister laughed. "Yeah that's what hour and a half classes will do to you."

Drue sighed. "No kidding."

Her sister pulled out of the parking lot and Drue closed her eyes again.

"So?" Her sister began, "any stories? How were your classes? How was band?"

"Classes were fine. Band was intimidating."

"Why?"

"Because everyone already knows each other. Even in my classes, they all went to Junior High together. They are all talking about old teachers and memories of last year. Stuff I don't know anything about."

"That will just take time. Soon you'll have memories to share."

"Yeah, I suppose. I really like the other clarinets. I think marching band is going to be fun. Intense, but fun. They take it very seriously. Do you realize we spend all semester preparing eight minutes of show?"

"Well that's band for you. But you compete right?"

Drue opened her eyes and looked at her sister excitedly. "Yeah they said next year we might even get to go to Indianapolis to compete in the National Marching Band competition. That means we'd be competing with marching bands from all over the country! How cool would that be?"

Her sister laughed. "You are such a geek."

Drue grinned. "Yep. They warned us about that. We will be called Band Geeks and we are supposed to respond, 'damn straight.'".

Stacey smiled at her sister, "I'm glad it went well."

"Me too. And how was your day, anything exciting?"

"No, nothing exciting, but I like all my teachers. I think it will be a good year."

"Yeah," Drue agreed. "Yeah it will."

She met him the first day of school. Well, she saw him the first day of school, but the memory is dim, because he didn't even stay through the class they had together: Math class; Freshman geometry. Hardly a romantic class, but then they were hardly romantic. Instead their conversations were sly remarks, teasing, and jabs at one another. She never considered it flirting, but then at that time she hardly knew what flirting was.

As for me, she met me that first day of school too, but I hardly doubt she'd remember. I was in the same math class, but they never noticed. I sat in the back of the room; I didn't make retorts, or talk a lot so I went unnoticed by the boy and girl who most dominated the class. The three of us were also in band together, but in a band of over a 100 people, a woodwind, horn player and drummer just didn't have much reason to associate.

Then one day in band rehearsal while he was sprawled out on the grass talking to a friend she came up to him. "Hey."

"Hey," he responded looking up. With a sly smile, his friend walked away.

She stood there for a moment awkwardly. He was clearly at home, sprawled out on the grass usually surrounded by friends. She looked down at him, shifting her weight from foot to foot. Finally she managed, "I didn't realize you were in band."

"Yeah, been here all year," he said easily. Band was his home, with both his sister and brother in the program he had been hanging around the band room for years. The people, teachers, setting and routine were second nature to him long before he had ever even entered High School. But after a moment's pause he realized that he too hadn't noticed her before. He looked at her again, and took notice of the clarinet in her hands. That must be why; he was in battery, there wasn't much association. And looking at her, standing there awkwardly, he smiled realizing that perhaps, unlike himself, she wasn't yet comfortable here. Perhaps, unlike in math class, here this spunky girl just melted into the background. He would have to change all that.

So it was that on the day of their first band competition when he found himself without a job to do, he looked around and spotted this girl. Drue, he had learned her name was. Drue something. He'd have to find out her last name. She sat in the midst of a group of people cutting flowers. Her hair fell in her eye and she reached up absentmindedly to tuck it behind her ear. He smiled, then walked over. "Hey."

She looked up and returned his smile. "Hey". She was surprised to see him, but happy, delighted in fact that he had sought her out.

They wandered…they talked. He learned her last name (she was wearing a name tag). He teased her. And when he ran away, she followed. It was nice, just wandering.

It was cold the night I met Drue. Cold, wet and miserable. We had just finished a three hour night practice and were waiting as the instructors went through their final talk so we could be dismissed. I held my trumpet, idly passing it from hand to hand, not really paying attention, wondering how I could possibly warm up my hands that felt numb on the cold metal. I could picture the warmth of the waiting band room. At last the Drum Major called us to attention and dismissed us. There was an audible sigh of relief from the band as we all turned to leave.

"That was awful," said a voice next to me. I turned to find Drue standing beside me.

"Yeah," I returned. "Practices really shouldn't be allowed to be that long."

"Agreed. I wonder if we wrote a petition if they'd listen." She raised an eyebrow at me.

I laughed. "Two freshmen? Hardly. Maybe the Drum Major,

everyone seems to like him."

"Personally," she said, leaning in just slightly and lowering her voice, "he kinda scares me."

I nodded seriously. "Me too."

"I'm Drue," she said moving her clarinet into her left hand and extending the other towards me.

"Chris," I said returning the handshake.

She smiled. "Nice to meet you."

I didn't know then what this girl would come to mean to me, or what an important role she would play in my life. I just knew that maybe she wasn't so bad after all.

"So how was your day?" Drue asked, falling onto her sister's couch and staring up at her.

Stacey looked up from the bookshelf where she had been searching for a book she needed. She shrugged. "Fine I guess. History was boring, we're watching a movie in Spanish, and we had a sub in English so James and I passed notes all through class which was fun."

Drue smiled. "What movie did you watch?"

"*El Norte*, it's okay, nothing terribly exciting."

"Did Sarah and Caitlin start talking to you yet?"

Stacey rolled her eyes and dropped to the couch beside her sister. "No, and I really don't know what to do about it. I mean, Drue, I tried to talk to them, I did. They want nothing to do with me, but I didn't do anything wrong!"

Drue looked at her sister, "I'm sorry Stace."

Stacey sighed. "Me too. And on top of that, everyone is all upset over this class rank thing."

Drue raised an eyebrow. "What class rank thing?"

"James and I are tied for first."

Drue's eyes went wide. "Stacey, that's amazing. Congratulations!"

Stacey smiled. "Thanks. But that's not the point. It has created all this unnecessary drama, which is so stupid, because there isn't anything any of us can do. James and I are taking like all the same classes anyway, so I'm not really sure what will happen...."

Stacey was going to save the world. Or, if not save it, then change it for the better. Drue had known this since she was little and Stacey had told Drue of her magical powers. From the day when Stacey told her baby sister that the twinkling in bubbles were fairies thanking Stacey for being the big sister, Drue knew that Stacey would do great things. Just as the rain was created to feed and give life to the plants, God had created Stacey to help fix the world and He had created Drue to help her sister accomplish this.

She can't remember if someone ever actually told Drue this was to be her life goal, it was just something that was always there, a destiny born within her. Even at fourteen Drue knew you didn't mess with destiny. If you were lucky enough to know God's plan for you, you certainly didn't just go and throw that away. It never even occurred to Drue to do so. Besides she liked fulfilling her destiny. Her sister was never short on love or affection and Drue felt useful.

So Drue would sit and listen as Stacey continued about her day, her life and her dramas. It never seemed weird that Stacey rarely asked Drue about her own day; Stacey's life was far more interesting than Drue's anyway. Drue much preferred her sister's stories to her own. Somehow those two years made all the difference. Stacey was preparing for college, had a boyfriend, her own car, things Drue could not even imagine. And so, like every day after school, Drue sat and listened until the dinner call was sounded and the two girls went to join their parents at the table.

3

September 28th

Dear Amor,

I think I am falling for Roger. He's in band with me. He's also in my math class (which means he sees me at my most hyper moments). Math is made up of a lot of our teasing back and forth. Mr. T. once accused us of flirting. We were just teasing. He makes me laugh. The bad part is he has a girlfriend, plus it's Abby. I love Abby. She's awesome and they make a REALLY cute couple. I don't want to like him. I just want to be friends with him. But the fact that thinking of him makes me happy and I can't wait to see him again, kinda worries me. I am promising myself it won't ruin our friendship, 'cause I love our friendship. He's so the best. I love him as a friend, but do I like him as anything more? The jury's still out. Though sadly I suspect yes. But the truth is I don't know anything about Roger. I don't even know his last name (I know it starts with an H). He has red hair (my favourite) and my favourite kind of haircut. He's about an inch taller than me. Very cute. Well I'm not going to dwell on him; in fact I will completely put him out of my mind.

I think he does like me as a friend. That's good. We'll stay that way, I'm hoping. I surely won't ruin it. I won't give the idea a 2nd thought (except maybe in you, if anything worth saying happens). Night!

Love, Drue

PS- He has a dimple Too!!! I feel like the typical teenager, staying up till midnight writing in her journal about some guy, God I'm pathetic!

"Do you want to be my bus buddy?" I asked as I walked up to Drue.

She hesitated for a moment. She had wanted to sit next to Roger, but then, what if he didn't ask her? She'd have fun with me, and I had asked her, so she smiled. "Ok."

I returned her smile even though I had a fairly good idea of what had just gone through her head. "Cool. Well then, see you later." And with that I walked away.

She returned to her book. A few minutes later Roger came over. "Hey."

She looked up, her eyes uncontrollably lighting up, "hey."

He plopped himself down next to her and lazily leaned over her shoulder. "Whata reading?"

She smiled, her heart picked up just slightly at having him so close. She looked at her book as if for the first time, turned it over to show him the cover and read with him, "The Subtle Knife," then as an afterthought, "Phillip Pullman" she said by way of explanation.

"Is it good?" he asked attempting his clearly unfamiliar small talk.

"Yeah, I really like it," she responded noting the lack of actual interest - I wonder what it is that he really wants? It came shortly.

"You want to be my bus buddy?"

Her heart stopped. "Yes." And then, damn it, "I can't." He raised an eyebrow. "Chris -" She motioned across the room, "just asked me," pause "but I really want to."

"Oh, no, don't worry about it. I'll sit with someone else," he said quickly.

"Alright," she said resigned, "but sit near us, k? So we can still talk. "

"Okay," he answered.

They sat across the aisle from each other. I sat at the window. She paid attention to me for about ten minutes before the focus turned to the pair of seats across the aisle. They talked, and I watched. People always talk about "love at first sight". I wish I could say that was the case for these two, everything would have been easier then, but unfortunately their relationship would never be easy. I'm not sure why. I don't know why it took two people in love so long to realize it; everyone else saw it, the way these two lit up when they saw each other. But they never saw it, not really. They saw joy in the eyes of the other, they saw laughter, they saw sarcasm, but they never saw love.

Around them the bus was loud, people were laughing and talking, singing and drumming; but these two, they didn't notice. When I bugged her enough she'd finally look over to answer my questions or give me some short response, but mostly they were in their own world. At one point he slept, and she turned to her diary.

"What are you writing?" I asked.

She looked up as if surprised to find me there. "Oh nothing," she said dismissively.

"Did you want to sit with Roger?" I asked.

"Nah, it's fine," she replied absently.

"What's Vegas like?" I asked.

"I'm writing…." she responded letting her voice trail off.

I took the hint and shut up.

We stood awaiting competition. This was always my favourite part. Competing, it's why we all did band. Not for the football games, but for this feeling, the adrenaline that came with performing at a competition, where every step had to be perfect, every horn snap, every pitch just right and then maybe you would get to walk away with a trophy. I held my trumpet nervously and looked around.

I saw him first. He was easier to find, having a huge base drum attached to him. Then a moment later I saw her. She was running up to him, she gave him a quick pinky power and then ran back. I didn't know what had gone on between them the day before. I saw in passing that they walked around all day, just talking. I had since been replaced as bus buddy. I smiled. I tried not to be hurt. I was not jealous; I was just waiting, waiting to be part of their circle.

In time it came. The three of us became a group. He didn't have that many friends and neither did we. The three of us, fit.

"We are a three-some," Drue said as she sat with her friend in art class.

"Drue!"

Drue rolled her eyes. "Not like that. Just we compliment each other well."

Her friend smiled. "That's because you are in love with Roger."

"Am not!" Drue countered. "He and Chris are my two best guy friends. How cool is that? I have two guy best friends. I've never had guy friends. They make me laugh. And they are friends too, kind of."

"You are too in love with him, Drue. Just admit it. Ever since you found out he and Abby broke up you've been gloating."

"Have not!" Drue was genuinely hurt. "I like Abby! You know I do. She was my first friend at this school."

"Yeah, but her and Roger were never right together. Trust me, even last year it was just weird." Her friend smiled. "You two on the other hand…." her voice trailed off.

"Ok, well can we please not get into this, you know he doesn't like me. "

"Oh my God Drue! You don't honestly believe that, do you?" She raised her eyebrows. Everyone knew these two would make it. Drue may be naive but surely she wasn't dense.

"He doesn't. Now can we drop it? Oh but guess what? He came and found me before school today. Found me! Can you believe it? It was so exciting!"

4

November 1st

Dear Amor,

People always ask if I'm happy at High School. I've begun to answer "Yes very", much to Mom's surprise. And I am. I don't really care for any of my classes, or teachers, but I can't imagine going anywhere else. I can't imagine having never met my friends, or never meeting Roger. I know it might not be forever. Will we be friends as adults? Probably not. Will we be friends all through high school? Maybe. For this year? I hope so. And all I can do is enjoy it while it's happening, because I know it won't last forever. But I'm not looking for a life long friend. I just need someone to look forward to seeing at school, a reason to get up in the morning, and Roger is that. So that's why I'm happy at High School, because I might not have found someone like Roger at another school, so I figure I'm pretty lucky.

Love always,

Drue Potter

I sat on the bus, bored. I wish we'd left already. It was 6am and people were slow moving. I took out a dollar and folded into a ring. I did it almost without thinking, like a doodle it was an extension of my hand more than a thought process. Just then Drue got on the bus her eyes scanning for two empty seats.

I waved to her from halfway down the bus. She smiled and started towards me. "Thanks" she said putting her stuff on the two seats in front of mine.

"Yep," I replied. I looked at the ring I had just folded. "Here, I made this for you." Realizing, as I said it, that it was true. I handed Drue the ring.

She took it and slipped it onto her finger admiring it lovingly, "Aw, Chris it's beautiful. Look," she said turning around and holding her hand up for me to see.

People were slowly getting on the bus. Some would come on, look for seats and then leave when they realized there were no longer two together. Other people found friends.

"Can I sit here?" A girl asked me.

I shrugged. "Sure."

No one asked Drue. Everyone knew who that empty seat beside her was for.

When Roger came up the steps of the bus he didn't look for empty seats, he came straight to where we were and slid in beside Drue.

"This seat taken?"

Drue smiled. "Now it is. Everything packed?"

He placed his backpack on the floor and leaned his head back closing his eyes. "Everything is packed."

"Good," she said. Then she paused. "Can I borrow a shoulder?"

He didn't open his eyes. "Of course."

She leaned on his shoulder and he rested his head on top of hers. That's how they remained as the bus began to slowly pull out of the parking lot. I, like the rest of the world, had been forgotten.

"How was your day today?" Drue's mom said turning to Drue as she sat down beside her daughter with a cup of tea.

Drue just shrugged. "Fine," she responded as she shuffled the deck of cards for a game of Rummy. "Nothing special."

"How was your Spanish test?" Her father called from the kitchen.

"Ok," Drue responded simply. "How was work?" She asked looking at her mother.

"Good, we had a baby named Drew today," She smiled at her daughter.

"Probably a boy though, huh?" Drue said raising her eyebrows at her mom.

"It's still a beautiful name."

Drue grinned. It was an argument she had been having with her parents since she could remember: Her insisting that her name was that of a boy, her parents insisting that it was perfect. However, in the end it didn't really matter since Drue loved her name.

Drue's Mom looked towards Stacey. "And what about you, anything exciting happen in school?"

"I am a National Merit Semi-Finalist," Stacey said casually, successfully stopping the game mid-deal.

Her mother looked up from the score sheet, her father came in from the kitchen with his glass of tea only half filled. "When did you find that out?" Drue's dad asked.

"Today," Stacey replied, "I got a letter. Because of my 1400 PSAT score, now I just have to do better than a 1500 on my SAT."

"Stacey, that's incredible. Good for you."

"Thanks."

"What is it exactly?" Drue asked.

"It's just an award, but only a few are given out in the whole country, and it looks really good on college applications."

"Cool," Drue responded, and began to deal again.

5

November 22nd

Dear Amor,

I just finished reading "The Luckiest Girl in the World". A good book. I'm not sure why I chose it in the first place, it was just there and I picked it up. Nothing particularly special about that. It's just. Well, it's strange to read about self-mutilation. I had never even known such a thing existed. I mean, eating disorders, well they surround you at every corner. They teach you about them in school, warn you about them, and tell you the warning signs to look for in yourself and your friends, but self mutilation? Who would even THINK to do such a thing to themselves? I'm such a wimp; I hate all types of pain. I can't ever imagine, WANTING to inflict such a thing on myself. I mean, the girl had like black outs. How could NOT cutting cause blackouts? Wouldn't you think it's the other way around, as if you fainted from the pain? I imagine it'd just be like a paper cut. But I hate paper cuts. They are bothersome things. Why would you ever wish for such nascence in your life? I don't know, the whole thing is just a whole different world to my own. I feel bad for those who must be in that world. I'm glad it's not me.

Got homework. All for now. Drue

He watched Drue out of the corner of his eye. She hurriedly brushed a wisp of dark hair behind her ear. She was bent over her notes, fervently writing, trying to take in the lecture that the teacher was giving. But he knew that she would still probably call him that night, needing help. Not because she wasn't smart, by no means, but because Geometry it seemed, was just not something she got. Like common sense, he thought with a smile. Yes, like the common sense that he was always teasing her about; her insistence to ask about the obvious or fail to see what was right in front of her. But what he could not understand is how such a person, so ditsy on the one hand, also understood so much. He had seen her writing in her journal; he had sat up with her at two in the morning as she plagued him with incessant questions. She was always thinking, using her writing as a way to get rid of some of the many thoughts that were always rolling around her head. She questioned her environment, the customs, and beliefs; she analyzed things and had this odd way of always having a profound thought in her head. And the most amazing thing of all was that she assumed all people thought like her. She didn't understand when he would reply "nothing" to her question of "what are you thinking?" She didn't understand that for him, to sit and think nothing, was not the impossible task it was for her. She glanced over in his direction and he quickly looked away before she could catch his eye. He didn't want her to know he had been watching.

So he sat there, half paying attention to the notes while watching this girl. Her blue eyes squinted up to see the board, one finger was in her mouth, a permanent adornment, while the other curled around her pencil. Her hair fell in dark ringlets; framing her face and making it look rounder than it was. She would often complain that she thought her head was square, but to him it seemed more like a heart. The two clips that held back her bangs were the peaks and from there it came around to meet at her chin. She had a few misplaced freckles across her nose, but for the most part her skin was smooth. She wore little makeup, but her cheeks, from a day in the sun, were rosy all the same. He never bothered to notice much what she wore, for her clothes were the average thing and nothing that might stand out or make her noticeable in a crowd. She liked this, this feeling of fitting in. He knew that she strove for it, and yet she never could quite give in to it. She was too happy to sit quietly and let others have all the fun. She would ask her question or give an answer; she would hide away from attention, cover her face with her hands if the spotlight ever sought her. She commanded a room with her presence, her smile and her laughter, but once she realized all eyes were on her, she would hide away, until she thought people had forgotten her. But people didn't forget her. She was new to the school, and already many people knew her, more than she even realized. And they respected her for she had a kind heart, and sincerely wished she could help everyone and anyone who was in need or hurting.

Roger smiled as he watched her, amazed that he had only known this person for a few months and yet already she had taken such a prominent place in his life. He would never admit it to anyone, but it was this girl that got him up in the morning and gave him something to look forward to in an otherwise monotonous day of school.

Drue bounced in her seat, unable to sit still until the bell rang, which would finally release us from our last class of the day.

"It's raining!" Drue whispered not too quietly to me.

"Congratulations?" I responded looking up from my paper distracted. We were meant to be working quietly on our homework but since the first raindrops had fallen ten minutes earlier Drue had closed her book and had been bouncing up and down restlessly in her seat, reminding me of the rain every minute.

"Drue, what are you doing?" The teacher had at last noticed that Drue was no longer even functioning under the pretence of working.

"Mr. T. it's raining out!" Drue tried to explain.

Mr. T. just stared back at her. "You still have twenty minutes of class. Please try to focus for at least that long."

Drue stuck out her chin defiantly. "You aren't supposed to do work in the rain Mr. T. You are supposed to dance in it. Now, surely we should be allowed to leave early so that we can take part in this tradition."

The rest of the class had stopped working. I heard a laugh from the back of the room. I instantly knew who it belonged to. So did Drue, who turned around in her seat in mock anger, "Don't laugh at me," she said pointedly to Roger, "I bet you've never tried it!"

"Drue perhaps you'd better leave," Mr. T. said realizing that no one was working on their problem sets.

Drue jumped up happily. "Really? Ok!"

Drue skipped out of the room. However, peace in the classroom was hardly re-established for every few seconds Drue could be seen through the doorway, twirling and dancing and skipping in the rain. Her arms were thrown out around her and her face was turned to the sky.

"Mr. T." said a girl in the back of the classroom, "may I be sent out of class too?"

"No," Mr. T. replied sternly, "Chris, will you go bring Drue back in please?"

I smiled. So much for that. I walked outside, "Drue!" She turned around grinning at me, "Mr. T. said you have to come in now."

She skipped over to me happily. "Fine. That was fun though. You sure you don't want to stay out? Just for a little?"

"You know they say that rain is the tears of the gods," I told her as we turned back to the classroom.

Drue just shrugged. "Well they aren't crying for me. So what an even better reason to rejoice!"

"Drue," Mr. T. was not smiling, "there is ten minutes left of class. Please go sit in the back corner, by yourself, and do not talk to anyone else."

Drue's smile faded. She picked up her books and sadly moved them from their normal spot next to me in the front, to the back corner of the classroom. She opened her math book and stared at it blankly. The class quieted down once more and we all returned to our work, but when I glanced back up at Mr. T. he was watching Drue, and smiling....

The bell rang. Drue slammed her book shut and jumped from her chair. "My Goodness, that was a long ten minutes!" She exclaimed.

"I really think there is something a bit wrong with you," I said walking over to her.

"Yeah, have you been smoking something without telling us?" Roger asked joining the two of us.

"No," Drue said defiantly, "you two just need to lighten up."

"This from the girl who can't handle being patted on the head?" Roger said performing the alleged action, which released a squeal of anger from Drue and set Roger off at a run out the door.

Drue grabbed her bag and followed. I walked more slowly behind. As I came out the door I saw the two of them a few feet ahead of me in the rain. Roger was poking and tickling Drue as she jumped about trying to fight back with playful hits and slaps. She looked up as I approached, "tell him to stop!" she whined at me.

I laughed and shook my head, "I am not getting involved in this one."

"Truce?" Drue asked then.

"Truce." Roger replied letting his hands fall to his side.

Drue grinned. She looked up at the sky sticking out her tongue to catch the raindrops in her mouth, and then she looked from me to Roger and back up the sky. "Yep," she said with a nod as if deciding something with great certainty. "If the gods are crying, it's definitely not for me." She smiled. "Come on lets go." She turned on her heel and began walking toward the parking lot.

We followed.

At lunch we would wander. None of us could sit still, so we'd eat then walk around. Not with any real purpose, just up and down the halls of the school talking and laughing. It was the most fun when it rained. Then I would watch as Roger tried to push Drue underneath all the gutters and she'd squeal with delight and fake rage. Between the two of us, sometimes we'd win, other times we'd let her get away.

On Wednesday's I had French club, but sometimes I would see the two of them pass as they did our walk without me. I would watch him poke or tease her and her squeals of delight would bounce off the walls like sunlight on water. Other days they would be deep in conversation as they passed my door and still others I would watch as they walked in silence, deep in their own thoughts just comfortable being near each other.

We never really talked about anything serious on those walks. We discussed band a lot, venting about instructors, or practice, or a particular scandal that had just taken place. We'd talk about how much work a particular class was, or Drue would come up with a life plaguing question and Roger and I would BS our way through some answer. Mostly we just teased. At night Drue would call me and we would talk for hours. She would start by asking about homework, or about my day, but the conversation always turned to Roger. I would listen as she told me her frustrations, her sorrows, and her joys. I would encourage her to have patience, myself wondering why he didn't just ask her out. And after a time of venting, she would calm down, hang up, and the next day would be the same routine.

Slowly, one day faded in to the next and the months passed.

6

February 12th

Dear Amor,

Chris is the sweetest guy. I love him. In a very different way than I love Roger, but still. Once Mr. T implied something might be going on between us and I laughed, not with Chris. Still I think I need Chris more than Roger. Chris has never let me down, never disappointed me. Yeah he's never made me as happy as Roger, but he can't; only the guy you're infatuated with has that great effect. It's nice to have someone in the middle who you can count on. Chris is loyal. I think I take advantage of him a little, I order him around some, but I think he also knows how much I need him. How lost I'd be without him.

Love always, Drue.

It was 2am. He was tired. He leaned his head back and closed his eyes.

"Wake up, wake up," she whispered in his ear.

He opened his eyes lazily and looked at the starry-eyed girl next to him. Her hair escaped her ponytail in small curls framing her face, her eye make-up was slightly smeared, a result of her resting her head on his shoulder. She grinned at him, "You mustn't go to sleep."

He rolled his head over to look at her, "Drue, It's 2am, that's what people do at 2am. They sleep."

"I know, but you can't go to sleep. Goodness where would the fun be in that?" She looked at him with cheerful naiveté, as if she really could not believe that anyone would want to be sleeping at such a time as this.

He smiled. "You are right. I'm sorry. Come here," he put his arm around her and she leaned into him. He wiggled his fingers mischievously. She let out a shrill squeal. "Shhhh," he grinned, "you'll wake everyone up."

"Stop, pleeeease," she giggled as she curled into him trying to escape the tickling, "Roger."

He stopped and looked at her innocently. "What?"

She glared at him, "when everyone gets mad for being woken up, I'm telling them it was all your fault."

He just shrugged. "And I'll deny everything."

She smiled. "What a great friend." She returned to her position resting her head on his shoulders. He let his eyes close.

He bought her a rose for Valentine's Day. She wouldn't accept a rose from anyone else. People would ask me why they weren't going out yet and I would always just shrug. "Beats me." By now, everyone knew they liked each other. Drue would walk into a new class and girls would smile at her. "We've heard about you." They'd say. Drue would roll her eyes, but she enjoyed it. She had never been gossiped about before, and now all of a sudden at this new school, where just a few months ago no one knew who she was people whom she had never met knew her name. She liked that when Roger was having a bad day it was she who was allowed to follow him. Once as she began to leave, she heard one girl ask, "Why does she get to go?" "Because," another girl explained, "Drue and Roger have a… special relationship." Drue smiled to herself as she went to find out what was bothering her friend.

Still, other times the gossip would drive her crazy. The "you and Roger as such a cute couple!" and "are you guys going out?" comments were incessant and they grated on Drue. They'd be sitting on the bus and the person in front of them would turn around. "Are you guys dating?" Drue would look to Roger, but he would not say a word. Just turn and look out the window, and so it was Drue who would have to respond.

"No, we are just friends."

"Why not?" The person would ask then, and Drue would want to turn to Roger and demand an answer to the same question.

But instead she would just shrug, "we are just friends."

The person would then turn around in their seat and soon Roger would turn back from the window and they would pick up their conversation once more, but these questions made it hard for Drue. It made it hard to be content with friendship.

Still, Drue remained patient, after all, what else could she do?

I sat at my desk staring at my computer screen wondering what exactly I was suppose to be working on. I picked up the phone and dialled her number. "Hi."

Her voice on the other end was distracted. "Oh hey. How are you?"

"Good."

"What you up to tonight?"

"I don't know yet, you?"

"Going to the play. Want to come?"

"*The Music Man*, again Drue? You've already been four times."

"I know, but it's really good, and it might be Stacey's last show, so I should go."

"Well maybe..." I began before being interrupted by Drue's soft cursing on the other end of the line.

"Shoot!"

"Everything okay?"

"No! Everything is not okay. The fabric for her dress is not sticking, and it looks just awful! What am I going to do! Shoot, shoot, shoot!"

"Ummmm... what dress?"

"I'm working on Stacey's card for tonight, and I just totally screwed it up. It was gonna be this great little dancing girl. Like you know those kinds where you pull the tab and the person moves. Yeah, well the dress won't stick, and the little pull tab isn't sliding right. Ah! This sucks."

"Ok, um, calm down. I think it'll be fine."

"No Chris, it won't. It's ruined!"

"Well I think your sister will forgive you if it's not perfect. After all she is your sister, and it is only one card."

Drue let out a small sigh, "I know, I just really wanted it to be perfect."

We were silent. I pictured Drue sitting in her room surrounded by art supplies, her fingers sticky from the glue. I smiled to myself. What Drue did for her sister would never cease to amaze me.

At last Drue spoke. "So why'd you call?" It wasn't mean, just surprised. As if Drue had just noticed I was on the phone.

"Oh, no reason."

"Oh. Ok. So do you want to come tonight?"

I shrugged. "Okay."

"Cool, I'll meet you there at seven thirty." And with that she hung up.

My mom dropped me off and I walked up the steps to the theatre. I didn't see Drue. I looked at my watch: 7:30 on the dot. That meant Drue wouldn't be there for at least another fifteen minutes. Sure enough at 7:50 Drue came running up the steps.

"Sorry I'm late. Traffic. Okay let's go in. We don't want to miss anything."

I laughed. "Drue you've seen it four times. What are we going to miss?"

She grabbed my arm. "Not the point. Let's go."

We walked in just as the orchestra was beginning the overture. We found seats off to the side and sat down. "Stacey dances more on this side, so you can see her better from here." Drue whispered to me as we slid into the row.

The show was good enough. For a school production of an average musical it was good. However to watch Drue you would have thought we had boxed seats on Broadway. She sat up perfectly straight in her chair, leaning forward just slightly, her head resting on her hands and her eyes completely riveted to the stage. She would sing along to the songs, and lose herself completely in the story. It wasn't until the lights came up for intermission that she once again remembered I was even there.

"So what do you think?" She asked me.

"Not bad."

"Yeah, I mean it's no Guy's and Dolls like last year. But still good, huh? Did you see Stacey? Wasn't she amazing… oh and after intermission she even has a solo in the first dance number! It's very exciting. You'll have to pay extra attention."

"Ok, I will," I assured her. We wandered outside and because there was nothing else to do we ended up at the concession stand. "Want something?"

Drue wrinkled up her nose. "I shouldn't."

"Ah, sure you should. What would you like?"

Drue pursed her lips and scanned over everything. I followed her vision until my eyes fell on a bag of homemade cookies at one end. I knew I could stop there.

"Cookies?" I supplied holding up the bag.

Drue's eyes went wide. "Yeah! Thanks."

I bought Drue a pack of cookies, and she ate them happily until it was time to return to the theatre. Then we went inside.

7

April 16th

Dear Amor,

I dream about him. Always the same dream, just with variations. We are walking around school, wandering as we always do when he suddenly turns to me and kisses me, or takes my hand, or tells the people we are walking with to go away. Then he turns and asks me out. Simply, no prelude, no explanation, just "do you want to go out with me?" and I always smile and turn away, just for a second, before answering very coyly and maturely, "yes". That is all. That is all that ever needs to be said, because we both know the rest. Then I wake up. I always wake up. And it's hard. Because all I want to do is go back to sleep, to that perfect universe where dreams come true. But instead I'm in reality, where we are just friends. And as nice as that is... Well, doesn't he know I like him? How can he not? Everyone else sees it. I just don't know if I'll ever get that dream. I'd really like it. I think he may be what has been missing in my life all these years. When I'm with him I certainly don't notice the emptiness, if it is there. I like him. I hope he sticks around. I hope he likes me too. I have to go to school.

Love , Drue

She picked up the phone. "Hello?"

"Hey."

Her heart skipped a beat.

"Hey," she responded.

His voice was tentative. "So how are you?"

"I'm good," she responded equally tentative, wondering why he was calling.

Pause. Just then her sister walked in. Drue remembered what she had wanted to tell him. "The drummers asked my sister how long we had been dating."

Silence. She continued. "Why did the drummer's ask her that Roger?"

"I don't know," he responded.

"But," she began, then took a deep breath. "So how are you?"

Later that night she called me.

"How could he not know! What the heck was he thinking? He's a drummer? Why wouldn't he tell them we aren't dating?" her voice picked up tempo and went up a pitch, "you think he told them we are dating? But why would he tell them that? You think that means he likes me?" She paused, and started over, calm again, unsure. "You think this means he might like me? Like do you think he said something? Oh, Chris, you think?..........." I just listened.

We were wandering at lunch. Our normal route, that took us away from the quad where all the popular people ate, through the halls, up near to where the gym was, but not all the way to the football field, after all the people who ate out there, well, we hadn't sunk to those levels yet. So we would turn, and wander taking the long route back to the band room and our territory.

"You want to come to my beach house this weekend?" I asked suddenly as there was a lull in conversation. My parents were borrowing the house from my cousin, and it was beautiful. I remember going there when I was little and I always thought there was something magical about that house. Each room was painted a different colour and decorated in a distinct taste of one of the many places my cousin had travelled over the years. So as you went from room to room it was like going to different countries, each with its own curiosities and surprises. My family had been spending weekends at the house on and off for my whole life, but never before had my parents allowed us to bring friends. It's what made this trip something special.

Roger and Drue looked at each other and then Drue looked back at me. "Sure I'll go. I mean I have to check with my parents, but probably. For how long?"

"We'd drive up Saturday, and then drive back Sunday. Just the one night."

"Ok."

We both looked at Roger. He shrugged. "Yeah, maybe."

I smiled. "Sounds good."

"Can I go? Pllllease?" Drue asked that night at dinner.

Her parents looked at each other, "I don't know." Her mom began, "You with two boys? I mean is that really safe?"

"Safe? Mother, what do you think is going to happen! Goodness. Besides Chris' parents are going to be there."

"And where is it?"

"I don't know, an hour south or so? I can get you all the information I promise."

"Is there going to be anyone else there?"

"Besides us? I dunno. But it's not like we are going to have some rager party or anything. For goodness sakes, guys, I don't drink, I don't do drugs, I just want to go and hang out on the beach for one night. I go away with band all the time!"

"I know, I know." Drue's mom sighed, "I just get worried."

Drue smiled. "Well don't be. I'll be fine. I can always call you, right?"

"Of course."

"So do you want to hear what happened to me today?" Stacey said piping in. Drue looked at her sister with a silent thank you. Stacey only smiled.

Drue moved the food around on her plate only half listening to her sister. A weekend away. With the beach, and her two best friends. Her stomach did a small turn, she hoped Roger could come. She hoped it'd all go smoothly. She hoped..... She smiled to herself, one step at a time....

8

June 15th

Dear Amor,

The school year is coming to a close. My freshman year of High School is done. I can't even believe it. I can't believe how much has happened! I mean, goodness, I didn't even KNOW any of these people this time last year. All these people who have become so important to me, and shaped me, and make up my life. So much has happened, so many memories! I am definitely not the same girl I was a year ago.

Roger signed my yearbook! And it was so nice. Ambiguous, but what in our relationship isn't? Still made me happy. He at least cares. We are friends. And that, is something amazing. He gave me his phone number and told me to: "learn it, love it, call me." Which means we'll definitely be hanging out this summer. What more could I want? Stacey is sunbathing by the pool, I think I'll go join her. Write more later!

Lots of love, Drue

"It's beautiful!" Drue squealed as we pulled up in front of the house.

"I know, pretty impressive, huh?" I responded. It was impressive, with its iron gates and tree lined driveway. Our car circled around the sculptured lawn which held a fountain and an array of brightly coloured flowers and pulled up in front of the Spanish style home. It looked like a house out of a movie, perfectly groomed and totally unlived in. And that was only the outside. I smiled. "You haven't seen anything yet."

As I gave them a tour of the two story house and its array of brightly coloured and eccentrically decorated rooms, Drue playfully hit me, "I can't believe I've known you for almost a year and you are just now bringing me to this place!" She grinned. "You really are a terrible friend. To think of all those times I wasted good outings on you while you had Hearst's Castle at your finger tips."

"I know, I'm a terrible person. Look at this," I opened the door, and Drue gasped. It was what the family called the den, but was more like a ballroom. The large room had only three things in it: two large sofas set in the middle and a bookshelf off in one corner. The rest of the room was completely open. The far wall, that ran the entire width of the house, was glass and overlooked the ocean at a breathtaking angle.

"Oh Chris!" Drue ran to the windows and pressed her hands up against it. Because we were on the second story this action gave the impression that it was possible to actually tumble over the edge right into the water beneath us. Drue took a step back.

I looked behind me to where Roger was standing wide eyed. He said nothing, but walked slowing into the room, his eyes wandering the length of the room. Finally, he nodded his approval. "Very nice," he agreed.

I nodded. "Yep, alright now that that's done. Let's go swimming. I'll show you where you can change."

We spent the afternoon laying on the beach; not exactly tanning, or reading or swimming, just laying and contemplating nothing, as teenagers are inclined to do. Drue lay with her head upon Roger's chest, completely oblivious to the conversation he and I were having. Life was perfect, right here, at this moment. She could feel his heart beat and his arm lay around her, as if to keep her safe. Roger and I were speaking nonsense but enjoying it, she could hear our laughter on the fringes of her consciousness. The sun played out its many colours on the soft waves and she wondered if there was any other girl in the world who was feeling what she was feeling just then. She wondered if there was any girl as lucky as her at that moment.

The phone rang. My mom picked it up. We heard her say "Hello"? Then a pause and then, "just a minute, Drue it's for you!" She called from inside the house.

Drue picked herself up. "Be right there!" She called as she ran into the house and took the phone from my mom. "Thanks." Then into the phone, "Hello?"

"Hi sweetie!" her mom's voice came through the receiver, "are you having fun?"

Drue smiled to herself, wondering if her mom could hear the smile in her simple. "Yeah."

"Did you want to come home? I can pick you up tonight if you'd like."

A moment of panic. Drue looked back to us laughing on the beach. Leave? Nothing in the world could make her want to leave. "Uh, no that's ok. I'm fine; Chris's mom can take me back tomorrow. Thanks though," she told her mom as nonchalantly as possible.

"Ok, that's fine. I just wanted to check in. Have a good time."

The panic was gone. Love for her mother replaced it. Her beautiful mother who was going to let her stay and enjoy this heaven for a few more hours. "Thanks mom," she breathed into the phone and then with a short, "bye, love you," she hung up.

She returned to the beach. Roger looked up as she

approached. “We decided your name is too short.”

Drue raised her eyebrows. “Too short?”

“Yeah, it should definitely be longer,” I agreed.

“For instance, we could add a ‘w’ because that would just make the “ow” sound stronger,” Roger put in.

Drue sat down cautiously as if scared we had actually gone crazy and might attack her. “O.....K....”

“Oh, and we could add a ‘g’ too,” I added.

“Why g?” Drue asked.

I shrugged. “It’s a good letter.”

Drue laughed. “Alright”

“How about ‘q’? Without a ‘u’ it’d be silent anyway.”

Roger nodded in agreement. “Perfect, that’s much better, Druewgq”

Drue just laughed. “Whatever you say.”

Just then Roger jumped up. “Come on we are going in the water,” he declared extending his hand towards her.

She looked up at him, wrinkling her nose. “Nah, you go. This is good for me,” she said stretching herself out on the sand. She wiggled her toes and grinned up at him defiantly.

He just shook his head, and pulled her up. “Oh no, if you are allowed to hold my hand in scary movies I’m allowed to hold your hand in the ocean.”

And with that he led her toward the sea. She squealed and tried to pull away as the first kisses of the cold water hit her toes, but he held her hand leading her into the crashing waves. She giggled and squirmed but he never let go, and so she remained, because, after all, when he was holding her hand, she would follow him anywhere.

We watched the sun set. Its rays played out on the sand like a kitten with a string, dancing and jumping from place to place as the light and clouds changed. Roger had gone inside to do his homework but Drue and I sat on the deck watching as day turned to night before our eyes.

I turned my head to look at her as she stared at the ocean. Her face was silhouetted against the sun that set behind her seeming to give her face a halo as she sat there in the approaching twilight. Her hair fell down about her shoulders, still wet from her shower, and she squinted at the setting sun, making her forehead furrow and the edges of her mouth turn up. Then they relaxed as she closed her eyes against the evasive light.

"I'm glad I came," Drue mused, her words just barely audible over the sound of the waves breaking.

I smiled, "I'm glad you came too."

She opened her eyes and turned to me, looking at me firmly. She smiled slightly. "Thanks Chris." It was formal, sombre, and yet I could hear the love behind it, the way you say thank you to a guest who came to a funeral or for a kind word on a bad day. Scared to break the sombre look on Drue's face, I didn't dare make a joke or ask a question. "You're welcome." I replied, because, that's all there was to say.

Then dinner was called. We got up and went inside.

Drue got up from her place at the breakfast table. "I'm going out to the swings!" She announced.

Roger raised his eyebrows but said nothing: I just shrugged, "Okay."

A few minutes later Roger and I walked into the backyard. Drue was just as she had promised, swinging herself up and down and singing happily. Her back was to us and I stopped at the door to watch. Roger stopped beside me. I turned to him, "So what do you think?" I asked.

"'Bout what?"

I nodded in the direction of the swings.

Roger watched the girl swinging up and down, "*I was thinkin', that I might fly today….*" Drue's voice came back to us from across the yard. Roger was silent, at last he sighed, "I don't know."

"She likes you a lot."

He nodded without looking at me, "I know."

"So, do you like her?"

He waited a long time before answering; I began to wonder if that was his way of telling me the conversation was over. At last he said, "I think so."

"So then, what's the problem?" I looked at him; he continued to stare at the swings.

"Because....," he searched to find the words, "because, just look at her Chris," he shook his head, "she scares the hell out of me."

And with that he started to walk over to where Drue sat. "I can't believe you really came out to the swings," he teased as he sat on the swing next to her.

She just looked over and grinned. "I told you," she replied as she jumped off and went tumbling to the ground.

He laughed. "Smooth."

"Very graceful," I added joining them.

"Thanks. I try," she laughed as she brushed herself off.

"Come on. We need to get ready to go."

She went skipping off in the direction of the house. She held out her hands and spun as she went, spinning and spinning. He followed one step behind until at last she stopped and he took her by the shoulders to steady her. I held back, watched, waited. I don't know what I was waiting for that day, but it never came. They never did look back. But then, it never was about me. How could it be? This, after all, isn't my story.

SOPHMORE YEAR: First Love

"There is no remedy for love, but to love more"- Thoreau

PRESENT DAY: APRIL

I walk into the restaurant and am surprised to see Drue waving at me from the counter.

"Hey," I say.

"Hello," she says closing her book. "I didn't know if you'd want a booth or a table so I waited."

I smile. "No matter."

"There okay?" She points to a booth by the window.

"Perfect."

"So how have you been?" She asks me as we slide into our respective sides of the table.

"Good. Nothing much is new."

"Well that's terribly dull."

"Yeah. And you? Excited about graduating?"

She looks up from the menu she's been glancing over; her eyes are wide. "No. I'm in pure panic Chris. I don't know what I want to do. I have a month and I have no idea. God, that's depressing."

I laugh. "Eh, it will work out. It always does."

She rolls her eyes, "I sure hope so. How's the book coming?"

"Not too bad. Got the first part done, now I just need to start sophomore year."

"Sophomore year…." The smile is inevitable; it is there before she realizes what she has done. She sits staring out the window for a moment just smiling to herself. Though she has too much pride to admit it, sophomore year still holds in Drue's mind this concept of perfection that she cannot let go of. She knows of course it wasn't perfect, she remembers the tears, but only vaguely.

"Sophomore year," I say again gently bringing her back to me.

She looks back from the window at me and shrugs, "yeah, ya know. What's important about sophomore year? It's that horrid phase when you are no longer allowed to claim ignorance and immaturity because you are a freshman and yet don't have the prestige and influence of being an upper classman," she pauses, "of course the work isn't so hard. That's good," she pauses again and shoots me a mischievous smile. "Yep pretty much your typical sophomore year."

"Drue." I stare at her.

Just then our waitress appears. We order, and I look back at Drue. "So you want to tell me about sophomore year?"

She purses her lips, and thinks for a moment. "Right," she begins at last, "Sophomore Year was that moment in life when circumstances and naiveté come together to allow you to live your dreams. Without inhibition, with complete trust and to find perfection in your life before you become too jaded to believe that perfection doesn't actually exist. That's what sophomore year was. It was my year of blissful perfection," she smiles, "I'm glad I was given that gift, even if it did take me years to recover from it." Drue is silent for a long time. I wonder if there is more. I can see Drue's mind working, calculating, but I am not sure if I will be allowed to be privy to these thoughts. Sure enough when she does begin again, it is just to look at me with a sad smile. "I dunno, what else is there to say?"

"Everything," I tell her.

She smiles.

9

October 12th

Dear Mary,

A new year, a new journal. And you finally have a name. (sorry it took nearly a month). You are named after the main character in my new favourite book. So, not a very exciting name (sorry!) But you have a noble namesake so be thankful for that.

Now then, it has been a year today that I found out Roger had broken up with Abby and I admitted to myself that I liked him. A year I've given him. For a year I've written about him in these pages, for a year I've put him in possession of my heart. But where did it get me? I'm in the same place I was last year.

I finally broke. We got together Saturday night. He paid for my dinner and yet outside of that it was just like we were friends. Basically I'm where I was last year at this time, in this horrible 'friends but...' stage and I'm tired of it. I hate that spot, it's getting me nowhere. So since I can't move forward I've decided to go back. I'm going to try very hard to get over Roger. Because then at least it won't cost me so many tears, at least then I'll have my heart back. But it's so hard. It's so hard to look at him and not see the guy I adore. But I'm working on it. This is depressing, I'm going to bed. In my dreams I get to hold Roger's hand!

Love always, Drue

He looked out the window wondering if this was the right moment to ask, or if there even was such a thing as the right moment. He stole a glance at her, but she didn't notice, her eyes were turned to the TV screen overhead. She was beautiful. Even here, on the bus in the middle of the night, after a long weekend of sweat, adrenaline, and exhaustion, she was beautiful. Even now, with her hair lazily pulled back in a ponytail save those few wisps that kept escaping in curls around her face, without makeup and in sweats and baggy shirt, she was beautiful; radiating simultaneously a calmness and energy that lit up the world around her. He took her hand in his.

She looked at him and raised her eyebrows as if to ask, "yes?" But she said nothing and when he remained silent as well, she smiled and contented herself with laying her head back on his shoulder and resumed watching. She had finally learned not to push him; that he would speak when he was ready. He knew how it drove her crazy not knowing where they stood at all times and yet here she was calmly waiting for him.

'Armageddon' played in front of them. A terrible movie he thought idly trying to focus on it, but there was no way to take his mind off the girl sitting beside him, the hand that he held. This girl who for the last year had so patiently, well, most of the time patiently, waited for him. Waited for him to get up enough nerve to do what he had wanted all along.

He took her other hand in his, "Drue? Will you go out with me?" He asked quietly.

"What?" She asked innocently lifting her head off his shoulder and turning to face him.

She hadn't heard him. He wondered if he had enough courage to repeat the question. Quickly before he had time to think, he took a deep breath and repeated, "will you go out with me, like officially?"

Her heart stopped. She had known it was coming, at least eventually, but now that it was here…. her mind was… blank.

"Yes" a smile crept over her lips. A pause. A shy look, "does this mean you're my boyfriend?" She asked in sweet naivety.

He smiled at her. "Yes."

She returned his smile. "Cool." Then she laid her head back onto his shoulder and snuggled into him. He wrapped his arms around her and held her for a long moment before wriggling his fingers playfully.

As expected she recoiled with a shrill, "hey!"

He continued to tickle her and she clung closer to his body hiding away from the hand that now encircled her. Her giggles echoed through the bus, but neither were paying attention. All they saw was each other.

She curled up against him feeling his body and for the first time since they met she did not wonder what it all meant for she knew, it meant he liked her. And as he encircled his arm around her to tickle and draw her in he thought only of how he could do this now, how it was his privilege because she was his. Just then the movie finished and the bus erupted in off-tune singing as the entire band sang to the credits, *"I could spend my life in this sweet surrender, I could stay lost in this moment forever,"* Drue's voice, from where she lay on his chest mingled in with the rest. He looked down at this girl. She was smiling and singing and watching the credits roll by, her eyes ablaze. She looked up at him and smiled, *"I don't wanna close my eyes, I don't wanna fall asleep, 'Cause I'd miss you, baby, And I don't wanna miss a thing."* He mouthed the words back at her, *"'Cause even when I dream of you, The sweetest dream would never do I'd still miss you, baby, And I don't wanna miss a thing."* Then he kissed her on the forehead, he had finally done it, he had won this angel.

They got off the bus a few moments later or had it been hours without their noticing? He smiled as he got up to stretch his long legs. She got up too and he followed her out holding onto her as she walked down the aisle, let them all see, let them know he had finally asked her.

The line in front of them stopped and he learned over her backpack. "We really should take six hour bus rides more often," he whispered.

She looked back at him and smiled. "Yeah, that would be nice."

She wondered if he could read her eyes in the dark bus, for in them was reflected her immense happiness. While everyone else was staggering off the bus into the two A.M. morning she was skipping. She was a little girl whose dream had come true. She did not know how long they would last, but she knew that while it did; it would be perfect .... and it was.

That was Sunday. I found out on Monday. They didn't tell me, but in school when we made our usual lunch-time walk they held hands and when he split off from us to go the other way to be picked up, he gave her a hug goodbye. That was suspicious.

Later, at her house we got ready for band together. It was nearly Halloween so we were wearing costumes to practice. She was doing my face paint. "So are you and Roger, like dating?" I asked.

She smiled, shyly, put down her brush and looked at me. Giving a slight nod. "Yeah."

"When did this happen?"

"This weekend, on the way back from Vegas." She was now looking at her hands, one still holding the paintbrush with green paint all over it.

"Why didn't you tell me?" It hadn't meant to sound so accusing. I was hurt. I was their best friend, shouldn't I have known?

"Well…" She paused for a moment, before continuing. "I just didn't know how to tell you. I mean I wanted to, it's just… you're not mad are you? You're still my best friend. I'd break up with him if you told me to, you know that right?" She asked quickly.

I tried to smile. "Don't be silly, I'm happy for you guys. You've liked him so long, now I don't have to listen to your venting all the time."

She laughed. "Yeah, well, we'll see. I don't even know if it will work out."

But I knew it would work out. It would do more than work out, it would be something special. And that meant that things for the three of us would never be the same again.

I wanted to be happy for them, I really did, but all I could think about was the sinking feeling in my stomach, the knowledge that despite what Drue said, I was going to lose my best friend or a least become the third wheel. But really, I was happy for them.

10

October 21st

Dear Mary ,

I really like having a boyfriend. Wow, I can't believe I just said those words! It seems so weird to call Roger my boyfriend. But I'm happy. I always imagined it would be good, but never THIS nice. Like yeah I get to hold his hand at lunch, and go up to him unashamed, but it's more than that. Like I get a hug now at the end of the day and he came up to visit me at every break at band (he NEVER used to come) and at the end of band when I was soooo cold he took my hand and warmed it up and put his arm around me. The little things. How did I get to be so lucky? I must have someone looking out for me. I told Chris, but that's it. Wow, it's still all a little surreal. Too good to be true, I'm a little wary. But truthfully this is worth so much. I'd give up so much for this feeling to last. I'm so happy.

- Drue

She opened her eyes and let out a sigh. She let herself bask in the calm of the dream, the security of knowing he was hers. Then reality crept up, and she began the process of bringing herself back to reality, of preparing herself for a day of seeing him and just being his friend. She sat up with a jolt. Wait, last Sunday he had asked her out. It was real now. Proof, she needed proof. She opened her journal that lay by her bed, and flipped through the pages, she smiled when she saw the entry. She fell back on her bed. It was real. He really was hers. It wasn't just a dream this time. She lay in bed consumed by this feeling while her alarm beeped incessantly reminding her of the school day that awaited her. She never wanted to move. She knew if she moved, she might ruin this moment. For at that moment, before all the little naggings of an average day set in, she was free to picture his face, to know that when she got to school she would be able to seek him out, she would be able to go up to him and to take his hand. What more did she need in this lifetime than that?

Still, she was going to get hurt. He had always been in control of their relationship; when they first went to a movie together, when he first called her, and when he asked her out. She knew she was always the one waiting for him, and that meant she loved him more. But someone always had to love more, and this time, it was her turn. Still, she reminded herself, she must be careful. She must protect herself, remember to keep her friends, and remember to stay true to herself, so that when he did leave she would be okay. She wondered when that would be, that he would leave. He and Abby had dated for five months, would they last that long? Hell, would they last a month? Yes they would last a month. After all, they had already been friends for a year, surely they could just continue on now that they were dating. Nothing had really changed all that much. However, even as she thought it, she knew it was a lie. Everything had changed.

She swung her feet off the bed, and padded over to the closet. She wondered how to tell her parents. It had been a week and she hadn't said anything to them. She was sure they knew, after all how could they not. Everyone in band knew after a day. She laughed, remembering how many people had come up to her that first night practice congratulating her, making snide comments. One of her friends had asked her how she was and then taken the question back commenting, "never mind, I know how you are." Her family, however, was different. She wasn't sure why, but she liked believing that they didn't know, that somehow this was her secret. She didn't want to share her joy; she wanted it all for herself. She had been waiting so long for this, now that she had it, she was not about to share.

She pulled her favourite shirt out of her closet. Yes, today was a red day.

Her mother gave a short intake of breath. Drue glanced over. Her mother was clutching the door handle tightly. "What?" Drue asked concerned, turning her attention back to the road, "what am I doing wrong?"

"Nothing, you are doing nothing wrong. I'm just nervous."

Drue glanced back to her mother who sat in the passenger seat of the mini-van one hand on the side of the door and the other poised as if to take the steering wheel from Drue at any moment. Her eyes bore into the road ahead and her brow remained just the slightest bit furrowed. "Well you are making me nervous."

"I know, I'm sorry," her mom said trying to steady her voice, "maybe Dad was right, maybe you should just practice with him."

Drue gave a quick turn of the wheel and instantaneously corrected it; however the car gave a sharp turn as if about to plummet into the shrubs beside the road.

"Drue!"

Drue grinned at her mother. "Just seeing if you were still awake." Drue turned back to the road. "Yeah, I think I'll stick to taking my lesson's from Dad."

"You guys are so cute." The comments started almost as soon as they became official. They were there before they were dating, but now she could bask in them rather than recoil from them. Her face would light up, she would stand up just a little straighter and she would respond "Thank you" in a proud voice. She was proud of him. She was ecstatic he had picked her, and though she knew she would be hurt, part of her also believed it would last forever. When people told her they would be voted cutest couple their senior year she would respond, "Well, lets not get ahead of ourselves." But in the back of her mind, she agreed with them.

Meanwhile I turned inward. I was their best friend, but they no longer noticed if I was in the room. They saw only each other. Her world became that of his, and even when she was with me, I knew that in the back of her head she was calculating the next time she was to see him. I watched them and knew that neither cared if I was there, knew that in fact they would prefer if I were not. So after a while I wasn't. I just left. I still played the part of the best friend; I was the one who told people that they were dating, answered their questions, and filled people in. It was as if I were their spokesperson, as neither noticed the world around them, why did they need to? There was nothing either needed except for each other. When they did begin to notice it was too late. She tried to care but her attempts were false and his insincere. They both acted out of obligation to me, but I knew when I left them they turned to each other and whether they discussed me or their plans for the evening, it was then about them, and what "they" were going do. I just did not fit into the equation anymore.

11

November 22nd

Dearest Mary,

It's nearly Thanksgiving! I love Thanksgiving. I'm not sure why. Everyone else always loves Christmas best, or their birthdays, or Halloween. But I have always loved Thanksgiving most. I like the presents at Christmas, and I like feeling special on my birthday, and well I just flat out hate Halloween (who could like a holiday totally devoted to dressing up, walking around in the dark and being scared?). Thanksgiving, Thanksgiving is the holiday about family. It's about counting your blessings, and thanking God for all the things you have in your life. And I have so many! I have my family, and my friends, I have Roger and a nice house, a great town, beautiful weather, and a whole life still to live and explore. What could be better than that? Yes, I really do have a lot to be thankful for! I better start my list.. don't want to be un-prepared when asked at dinner!

Gotta run. Lots of love! Drue

She took his hand in hers, tracing the outline of his fingers with her own. "We did good today."

He grinned at her. "Like hell we did."

She leaned her head on his shoulder but before she had time to close her eyes he lifted her chin and began kissing her.

She began to giggle. He pulled back and raised an eyebrow at her. "What?"

"I can't believe we've become one of those couples," she said covering her mouth with her hand to suppress the laugher.

"One of what couples?"

"The kind that make out in the back of the bus! God we are awful!" She buried her face in his shoulder.

He put his hand on her head smiling. "Yes, well there are worse things." He lifted up her head. "And if you've already judged us as one of 'those' couples, we might as well live up to it, right?" He leaned over to kiss her but she erupted in giggles once more. "Well if that's how you want to play," he said putting his arm around her and tickling her so that her giggles turned into squeals.

"No Roger, stop I'll be good. I swear, please, stop." She reached up and kissed him. He stopped. She grinned, "I win."

"Nah," He shook his head, "I win," he said kissing her, "I always win."

And so Roger and Drue became one of those notorious band couples that made out on the back of the bus as it drove through the night while the rest of us respectfully pretended not to notice. Or care.

It was lunchtime. I looked around for somewhere to sit. I saw them sitting on the far side of the field, their heads were together talking. As I watched she threw back her head laughing, he leaned over and started tickling her. I sighed, I couldn't sit there. I walked over to some other friends and sat down.

"Hey."

"Hey," they responded, "you aren't sitting with Roger and Drue today?"

I shrugged. "Doubt they will notice."

One of my friends looked at me with pity, "there is always a honeymoon period. You just have to give them a few weeks."

My voice was flat; "it's been a two months." I said.

"Oh." The girl looked across the field, Roger got up extending his hand to Drue, she got up taking his hand and they headed off to wander, without me. The girl looked back at me and shrugged. "I'm sorry. I'm sure if you just give them time."

I shrugged. "Doubt it. Probably wouldn't even notice if I killed myself."

"Now you know that isn't true. They would not only notice but care very much. As would a lot of people."

I shook my head. "No, no they wouldn't. I'll be standing right there, and they won't even notice anymore. All they see is each other."

Drue came in the door to find her sister standing in the hallway. She was crying. In her left hand was a large envelope and Drue knew it could only mean one thing. "You got in?" She asked, holding her breath.

Her sister nodded.

Drue's bag fell to the ground as she threw her arms around her sister. "Stacey, oh my God, congratulations! That's amazing, I'm so happy for you!"

Stacey beamed back at her sister. "Me too, I mean, thank you, wow, I'm in shock."

Drue laughed. "Yeah I can imagine. I knew you could do it." Just then Drue's mom walked in, Drue turned to her excited, "Mom, Stacey got in!"

Drue's mom broke into a wide grin. "Honey that's incredible. I'm so proud of you," she said giving her daughter a hug.

That night they all went out for a celebratory dinner, and that night Drue was able to stop praying that her sister would get into Stanford. Instead, she thanked God, thanked him from the bottom of her heart for it seemed both her and her sister had gotten their dreams that year. Drue could think of nothing better.

We sat in her room. Drue and Roger sat on the bed pouring over the notebook they held between them. I sat on the floor across from them, wondering if they even noticed I was in the room.

"What do you think?" Roger raised his eyebrows at Drue. She glanced over the book, crossed out a few lines then nodded back.

"Sounds good. Here Chris, read this, what do you think?"

I took the notebook from Drue. It was the opening of the paper we were meant to be writing together but on which I had so far done nothing aside from a few spelling corrections and grammatical errors. Such were the things I was now searching for, not even bothering to pay attention to the content. "Looks good," I said handing it back.

"You didn't even read it," Drue countered taking it back from me.

"Yes I did," I responded, though of course I hadn't. I knew they didn't want to know my opinion anyway. I returned to the paper I was cutting. I was making cut-outs of their names: first Roger's, and now Drue's. Cut out, perfect, and totally separate from the rest of the world.

Drue stared at me, watching me cut in silence for a long moment. I wondered briefly if she did care, if maybe she would ask me to write some of the paper, or to join them on the bed to sit and jointly write paragraph by paragraph as they were doing. But then the moment passed and she just sighed returning the notebook to Roger. "Alright, if you say so."

They returned to their writing, I returned to my cutting and we did not speak again for twenty minutes. Then the doorbell rang. Drue glanced at the clock and jumped up. "Shoot!" Roger and I both looked at her waiting, "I have a driving lesson. I totally forgot." Drue bent over to pull on her shoes. Roger and I began to look around us awkwardly.

"Um, Should we go?" I asked finally.

Drue was looking for her coat and glanced up from the search surprised to still find us there. "Oh, uh, no. It's only an hour. You'll be okay here, right? I mean I'll be back soon and besides," she added raising her eyebrows with a smile, "maybe you'll get some work done while I'm gone." She found her coat then and put it on running to the door, "I'll be back soon!" She called from the hall. We heard the front door open and then the car pulled away.

Roger and I stared at each other in silence. Then Roger shrugged and returned to the notebook. I returned to my cutting.

"I can't understand why no guy wants me. I mean it's not like I'm a bad girl."

"It's not that guys don't want you…"

"No, just not for more than one night. Why can't I find more than that?"

Drue walked to the sink to wash her hands looking behind her in the mirror as she did so to watch the two girls who had been talking. The girls were both strikingly beautiful. The one, a perfect specimen of a California beauty, dressed in Bebe and Abrocrambie, her tan skin the perfect shade against the blond hair that fell about her face. The other was tall and dark. Her features were exotic looking, with striking blue eyes against black hair that fell to her waist. How jealous would these beautiful girls be of her if they knew she had what they dreamed of? Drue looked at her own reflection in the mirror, her plain face and frizzy curls. She knew she would never be as beautiful as these girls, never as thin, or as striking looking; no one would ever stop and give her a second glance as she passed them on the street, and yet, she was in a relationship that these girls only dreamt of. Drue smiled to herself as she dried her hands, she was lucky, that was all there was too it.

Drue walked out of the bathroom. Roger was waiting for her. She threw her arms around him.

"What was that for?"

"I was beginning to take you for granted."

He kissed her, "Well you can take me for granted any time you like."

She grinned, "I don't plan to."

He took her hand. "Shall we?"

"Yes, Lets."

I threw her a surprise party. It wasn't hard. Drue sat so absorbed in her new boyfriend we could practically talk about it right in front of her and she wouldn't notice. It was my last attempt. I somehow had this belief that if I did this wonderful thing for her she'd notice me again; she'd realize what a good friend I could be.

It didn't work. When we all said "surprise" it was Roger's arms that she sought in stunned joy, it was to him that she said thank you over and over again. There was nothing I could do but stand by and watch. She was happy at least. I had done that much.

And Drue was happy. She had never felt more loved, accepted, or happy than she was on the day she turned sixteen. As she blew out her candles she made the same wish she had made every year since she was ten years old, but this birthday she closed her eyes and wrinkled up her forehead and wished extra hard because she knew this year her wish probably never would come true. How could she ever be happier than she was right at that moment?

12

February 6th

I hope I never forget this night, or at least this feeling, of awe. Like the night he asked me to homecoming, or kissed me, or asked me out. I kind of knew they were all coming, but that doesn't make them seem any less surprising or exciting or amazing. I still can't believe he's mine. I don't know if I'll ever be able to believe that.

- Drue

He held her. "My angel," he whispered in her ear, "see there's your halo, it's a wonder you don't get hit by it, the cumbersome thing."

She giggled.

"God you are beautiful," he said it under his breath, more to himself then to her.

"Please don't," she whispered back. They were lying on his bed after dinner, and she was so content in his arms, just laying, not thinking, not worrying, just being. Why did he have to go and ruin that?

"Don't what? Tell you you're beautiful? That you are perfect?"

"Yes, don't lie to me."

"It's not a lie Drue, you must believe me."

But she couldn't. To her she would never know that she was pretty, she would never see herself as others did. Instead she saw only someone who was not as good as her sister, not as smart, not as beautiful, not as talented. And amazingly this didn't bother Drue. She wasn't depressed or even saddened by it for it was all she knew, it was fact. She was average. She would never be the girl that all eyes turned to watch when she walked into a room, and she would never be first, but that was okay, too many eyes made Drue nervous, and when you were average no one gives you a second glance.

"Drue you are beautiful," Roger whispered again in her ear.

Drue hit him, not hard, but for Drue any act of violence was rare and far between. Roger pulled back. "Roger Hero you stop that right now," she said. She was serious without a hint of teasing or sarcasm. "Lying is a very bad habit."

Roger gave in. He knew he would not win and so he contented himself by wrapping his arms around her and tickling until she squealed for him to stop. Whether or not Drue saw it, Roger knew she was beautiful. She was beautiful in the way that you might walk past her in the hall without noticing, but then one day in class without meaning to your eyes would drift to her face and you would study it absently. The curve of her jaw, the way her eyes lit up when an idea rushed through her, the way her smile took over her face when she laughed. And all of a sudden you'd realize this girl was beautiful. Her eyes a clear lake, her lips a perfect heart and her cheeks the colour of roses in spring. From that day forward it was impossible to walk by her in the hall without noticing the curls that had escaped her ponytail to perfectly frame her face or the way her earrings danced as she laughed with her friends. Drue was that kind of beautiful, the kind that you could never quite shake from your mind once you discovered it. Roger stared at her wondering how it was that she could not see that, wondering if he could make her see.

"What are you thinking?" Drue asked then.

"Ummmmm." He was thinking how he could care about, no love, someone so much. Yes, he loved this girl. The realization came as a shock. But there it was. He loved her. He loved her laughter and her smiles, he loved how she danced in the rain and sang to the stars, he loved that she cried at sad love songs and was scared by cheap horror films, he loved that she could talk for hours about nothing and couldn't sit still for more than ten minutes at a time. He loved that she wasn't afraid of her intelligence, he loved that she walked into trash cans and couldn't spell, he loved that she could laugh at herself. He loved that she picked him. With Abby he had been scared of the day when he would get tired of her, but with Drue he didn't fear that day, instead it was the day that she would get tired of him that he feared. The day that she would wake up and realize she could do better.

Roger looked up to find Drue still staring at him waiting for his answer. She brushed a piece of hair out of his eyes and raised her eyebrows expectantly.

"I was thinking, Miss Drue Potter," he began smiling up at her, "that I love you." There it was. Just like that, the words that he had not uttered to anyone in so long were now hanging in the air.

Drue didn't respond right away, instead she cocked her head first to one side and then the other, looking at him, no scrutinizing him. Finally she said softly, "I think I love you," a pause and then, "how do you know?"

He smiled taking a finger and tracing the outline of her face. "You just know," he answered, "you just know."

She stared at him again her brow wrinkled and he smiled watching her work out this knowledge in her head. Then she gave a slight nod. "Yes," she said, "I love you." Then her forehead relaxed and her face broke into a wide grin. "I love you too," she repeated and kissed him.

He held her to him savouring the moment, remembering this single second in time when the world perfectly aligned itself around them and everywhere there was peace.

Drue looked at the clock and jumped up. "I have to get home. I said I'd be home by nine."

He pulled her back. "That means you have twenty whole minutes."

She fell back into his arms and tried to struggle free. "I have to drive home. You don't want me driving unsafely now do you?" She smiled up at him sweetly.

He buried his face in her neck. "No, but I want you to stay here."

She laughed. "So do I, but I really must go."

"I won't let you," he replied defiantly, "I'm keeping you here forever."

"Yes because my parents would really go for that."

"We won't tell them."

"Great, so now you're a kidnapper?"

He shrugged, still holding her in his arms. "Eh."

She giggled, "Rogeeer."

"If you go, I won't kiss you ever again," he tried.

She just looked up at him and without undoing his hands she turned around and kissed him. "I win," she said proudly a smile covering her face.

"Damn." He lessened his grip. "Let me walk you out at least."

He walked her to the door where she turned and gave him a goodbye hug.

"I love you," he whispered in her ear.

"I love you too," she returned the words that already seemed natural, appropriate, and perfect. "I'll see you tomorrow." And with that she turned and left.

Drue got into the car and looked at the clock. Eight fifty-five, damn, she'd be late, again. Still, she thought with a smile, Roger had told her he loved her, surely that was worth being late. Her parents would just have to understand.

He watched her get into her car and then he turned around and headed back into his room.

It was only a few moments later that my cell phone let out a piercing beep from across the room. I put down my math homework and went to retrieve the offending object. As I picked up the phone "One New Text Message" flashed across the screen giving reason to the obnoxious sound. I opened the message. "I finally said it," I read out loud. It was from Roger. I smiled. "About time," I texted back. Then returned back to my homework.

13

March 1st

Dear Mary,

I used to have only one hero, only one person to live for, only one person to please. Then I grew up and all these other people became important, like me and Roger. Then Stacey told me not to forget who I was, that she didn't like this new me, so then I thought of who I used to be and who was important to me then: Mom, Dad, Stacey, Chris. I remember once asking Stacey why it was that she didn't enjoy the family's company anymore. She said it just wasn't where she was happiest, I remember being so hurt, failing to see how that could be true. Now I understand, but I don't want to. I want to fight it.

Then there's Chris who seems so sad. Sadder than I've ever seen him, it started when Roger and I got together. I don't know how to make him happy. And I don't know how to balance that with keeping myself happy. Recently he's begun asking people if he should kill himself. It's in jest, yes, but it's still morbid. Roger and I are both worried about him. I decided we should do something to show him we care. We've excluded

Chris from his two best friends. It seems so mean. But what should I do, whose happiness is more important, mine or Chris'? Then there is Roger, and my parents, and Stacey. How do I please everyone? I failed my Spanish test today because I was kissing Roger last night when I should have been studying. I let my parents down. Chris told Roger something and when Roger wouldn't tell me, I got angry. I let Roger down by forgetting the ever so important rule - "don't expect anything of him" and Stacey, well, I'm sure she wouldn't be very proud of me right now. So who do I choose? How can I choose? How do I make things better? I like being happy, but it seems to be happy, I have to hurt so many people and I don't want to do that, but don't I deserve to be happy?

- Drue

As always when they rehearsed with Battery her eyes wandered away from her music to search out his. She looked up and tried to catch his eyes and smile even though she knew he couldn't smile back. To break his stern glance would be against protocol, but sometimes she'd get a raise of the eyebrow or a slight nod of the head so she knew he saw her.

He looked up and saw her staring intently at the instructor, a slight frown on her forehead and a single tooth showing as she bit her lip in concentration. So cute, he thought. Then he had to shake his head, clearing his thoughts not to loose his place in the music. She really was rather distracting.

She caught his eye. She knew it and her face lit up, a smile reaching from ear to ear and her eyes danced with joy. What would it be today, the eyebrow? The nod? Would she be rewarded with something?

Before he could stop himself he broke into a smile. He couldn't help it, it was just a glimmer of the huge smile she had on her face, an instantaneous reaction to finding her grinning at him. A second later his smile was gone and he looked away with consternation. He pasted the drummer's scowl back on his face with new determination. How dare he loose concentration like that! He must just not look at her anymore he scolded himself.

Her smiled had grown, her music completely forgotten for the moment. She had won. She had beat band's influence over him. She had, for one precious moment, been more important than the hard core image band demanded of its drummers. Yes, he must really love her. Victory was sweet.

She would try not to gloat about it too much later.

"This town really is full of beautiful people isn't it?" Drue mused to herself, as she turned her smoothie slowly in her hands.

"And that is why you fit in so well," Roger said, leaning over kissing her.

She playfully hit him with a roll of her eyes. "Yeah, riiiight. Because clearly I'm tall, blond, thin and perfectly tan all year round," she shook her head. "I really need to go on a diet."

He got up. "You're perfect. Now, I gotta run. My parents are expecting me home for dinner. I'll see you guys later." He stood up kissing Drue's forehead, "call you later. Love you."

"Ok. Love you too," she said smiling up at him. He left. We remained. The sun was setting and the spring breeze was cool against her bare shoulders. She looked at me from the corner of her eyes, I looked straight ahead. We didn't really have that much to talk about anymore.

She sighed. "So what's new with you?" She asked at last.

I shrugged. "Not much."

"Right."

We sat in silence.

"What can I do?" She asked suddenly.

"What's wrong?" I looked at her blankly. "I'm not stupid," she went on, "but I just don't understand why you can't just get over it and be happy."

"Well, I can't exactly just 'get over it', sorry," I responded.

"Why not Chris? What is so wrong with the world?"

I shrugged.

"I'm not going to dump him you know. If that's what you

want. I love him. And he makes me happy."

"It's not what I want," I responded, "but at least you offered when you first got together. I was more important to you then."

"Well. Now..." her voice trailed off. She knew better than to finish the sentence. She took a deep breath, and tried again, "I'm just saying. I'm still here. I know it's not how it used to be. But I haven't left." She looked at me. I looked back, but I knew she had. And not just because she wouldn't break up with him for me anymore, but because she had no idea of what I was going through. Drue didn't understand depression; she didn't understand the dulling of colours, and the inability to see the bright spot in a dismal day. She didn't know what it felt like to wake up in the morning and dread the idea of movement. She didn't know what it was like to hate yourself so much that you could no longer validate why you deserved to have friends. Drue really believed I could just 'decide' to be happy, and then all would be right again.

I got up. "I should get home."

She nodded. "Okay." She got up, and we stared awkwardly at each other, wondering what had happened to our friendship, where exactly it had gotten lost. Then we turned and went in different directions down the street.

I walked slowly down the road. Drue was right; this town really was filled with beautiful people. It was a picture perfect Southern Californian town, with palm-lined streets, and brick lined shopping malls. There were push carts full of merchandise and over priced coffee shops on every corner. The malls held only the trendiest of stores, and the people dressed in only the latest fashions, discarding last years clothing to the thrift stores and the Salvation Army. I would never fit in here. Neither would Drue, and Roger, well he would later, but not at fifteen, and it was what brought the three of us together. Our refusal to align ourselves with exactly what was fashionable or trendy preferring instead the wholesome forms of entertainment, the more comfortable forms of dress, and the more substantial ways of eating. The problem was, without the other two beside me, it no longer felt like a social choice, just alienation.

"Drue please come. You owe that much to Chris."

Drue sighed and said nothing but she followed her friend down the hallway. She didn't want this meeting, she didn't like the whole idea of it, she didn't understand the point of it, and she knew somehow that she was going to be blamed for everything.

"Hi Drue," Ms. Simon said when Drue walked through her door. "How are you?"

Drue shrugged, "I'm fine. How are you?"

Ms. Simon smiled. "I'm good, thank you. Take a seat."

Drue looked around the empty classroom, paused for a moment and then chose a seat half way back. She jumped up onto the desk so that her legs hung off the edge. Ms. Simon sat behind her desk at the front of the room. "Do you know why I had you come in today?"

"To talk about Chris," Drue returned.

"Do you know what is going on with him Drue?"

"I know that he is depressed." Drue swung her legs absently.

"Yes, he is very depressed. And I don't know about you, but I'm worried about him."

"I am too," Drue said lightly.

"What are you doing to help him?"

Back and forth, back and forth, Drue's feet went under the desk.

"Drue?" Ms. Simon pressed.

Drue looked up and met Ms. Simon's eyes. "I tried," she said then, "I tried everything I could think of. I called, I wrote letters, I invited him to do things, I tried to talk to him, I tried to get him to go to counselling. None of it helped, and I'm out of ideas, I'm done trying."

"You can't just give up on him."

"I can, and I am," Drue said with finality. "I don't care anymore."

"You have to care," Ms. Simon told Drue, "he is your best friend." It wasn't a question.

"Well I don't," Drue spoke softly without expression.

"He may kill himself Drue. Did you know that? He's that depressed. And if he does, it will be your fault. It will be your fault if you don't do anything."

"Well I just don't care anymore," her voice held a degree of anger in it; "there is nothing more I can do. He doesn't want my help. So if he wants to kill himself, then let him. I don't care." And with that Drue jumped off the desk and walked out.

Once outside her pace slowed and she shook slightly as she tried to catch her breath and keep herself from crying. She prayed to God that Ms. Simon was wrong, that I would be okay and she continued to pray every night. However, to the outside world, she kept her word. After that day she no longer seemed to care. She stopped calling, stopped reaching out. She'd look away if I walked by.

I bought her a present; I wanted to tell her I was sorry, I wanted her to know I hadn't meant to cause her pain. But she wouldn't accept my gift. She just stood there and stared at me, refusing to take it from my hands. Roger was with her so he took it and as I left I heard him coaxing her to accept it, "he's your friend Drue, take the gift and letter. You owe him that. Just read it."

I don't know if she ever took it. If she did, she never let on.

14

March 17th

Dear Mary,

The other day I told Roger I wanted to be invited to his wedding. He wrinkled up his forehead. "Don't say things like that Drue." He said. I just laughed, "What that we aren't going to get married? Honestly Roger." "I know." He responded, "I just, don't think about it, I guess." But that seems funny to me. I mean, we are sixteen years old. What does he expect? Yes, I love him. He is definitely the first love of my life, but the last? Surely not. And I do want to be invited to his wedding. I am curious to meet the girl Roger ends up with. I guess because I so can't picture it. Hm, ah well. I won't bring it up again.

All for now! Drue

He paced up and down her driveway. He played with the roses in his hand. He wanted everything to be perfect. Just this once he wanted to be perfect for her, show her he loved her, despite all her fears, show her he cared, and that he would continue to care. He wished he could go in already. Drue's parents had told him to wait until nine, saying Drue was sick and needed her sleep. He stared at his watch, ten minutes to nine, ten more minutes! The waiting was killing him!

Drue's mother came to the door. He froze, hoping she wouldn't yell at him for being early. But she only smiled, inwardly laughing at his boyish nervousness, at his desire to obey her wishes and yet unable to contain his excitement. She held open the door. "You can come in if you want."

Drue lay in her bed wide-awake. She had been up for nearly an hour, but didn't want to leave. She wanted to be right here, asleep in bed when Roger came for her. Or at least, she hoped that was what was going to happen. He didn't tell her exactly that his plan was to wake her up and take her to breakfast, but she guessed as much from his vagueness on the phone the night before. Of course she could be wrong, and then be lying here in her cutest pyjamas for no reason at all. After all if he was going to come, wouldn't he have come already? She rolled over and looked at the clock, a quarter to nine, who wakes someone up at a quarter to nine? Who was still asleep at a quarter to nine?

Just then she heard someone in the hall. Ah, her parents were up. As the door opened she rolled over to say good morning. And there, standing in the doorway, holding a bouquet of red roses, was Roger. He was framed by the door and the light from the hall glowed around his tall frame. She thought for a moment that it was a dream; a perfect, amazing dream, just as she had been imagining a moment before. Then he moved from the doorway and she knew it was real.

"Good morning," she said, a smile playing across her lips.

"Good morning," he responded, moving to her bed. He sat down. "These are for you." He handed her the roses.

Her smile broadened. "Thank you".

"Happy Anniversary." He leaned over and kissed her. A gentle kiss, a good morning kiss.

"Happy Anniversary," a pause, then, "I thought you were in

my dream."

"Nope, I'm for real."

"So, what now?"

"Now we go to breakfast," he said, taking her hand and helping her out of bed.

"Ok, just give me a minute to get dressed."

He smiled and shook his head playfully. "Nope, you have to go just like that."

Her eyes widened, even though she had suspected as much. "Can I at least brush my teeth? Since you have to talk to me and such."

He laughed. That was her biggest concern? "Yes, you may brush your teeth."

She smiled. "Thank you!"

She ran off to the bathroom, leaving him in her room alone. She hadn't seemed as surprised as he had expected and hoped, but she had seemed happy. Yes, she had been happy, he was sure of that.

He looked at his watch. How long had it been? Five, ten minutes? How long did it take someone to brush their teeth?

He walked to the bathroom. Drue was brushing her hair. So much for her not caring about appearance. "Hey, the deal was teeth only"

She looked at him guiltily. "But I had bed head," she said in a small voice.

He laughed. "Alright, let's go." He took her by the hand and led her out the door.

As they walked by the kitchen, she leaned in to where her parents were standing at the counter talking coffee in hand.

"Roger and I are going out for breakfast."

Her mother smiled. "Aren't you going to change?"

Drue shook her head. "Nope, Roger won't let me. I got to brush my teeth though! But that was all," she explained happily.

"Alright then, have a good time."

"Of course." Drue kissed her parents goodbye.

Her parents smiled as they watched their daughter leave. She was happy. In every move of her body they could see her happiness. She smiled, skipped, sang and was more talkative now than they had ever seen her. They liked Roger. They liked him as a boy, and they liked him for the change they saw in their daughter. Their only hope was that of any parent for their daughter, they just wished that she would not be hurt. But then, after six months, no matter how much any of us wished that, even Drue knew it was inevitable.

15

June 16th

Mary,

Stacey just left for Prom. She looked so beautiful. Like a princess. And James picked her up, with roses, and aw it was amazing. I hope I have a Prom like that. I wonder if I'll go with Roger. I wonder if we'll still be together then. I hope so. It would somehow only feel right with him. But then, Prom is still two years away, so it's impossible to say I suppose. I wish I could be going to Prom. Roger almost went, with a friend of his sister's. That would be so much fun, to go. But maybe it'd make it less special. Like maybe you are only supposed to have one Prom, that way it can be perfect. I hope Stacey's is perfect. She deserves that.

Night. Drue

The day was beautiful. Drue wore a gold dress; she had borrowed it from her sister's closet that morning and Drue liked the way the silk brushed against her skin. She felt pretty. It made her smile and she turned her face up to the sky to feel the warmth of the sun. She reached her destination and walked in.

The band room was bustling with people. Everyone was dressed up and the seniors, in their blue and red robes, were racing around taking pictures, ushering parents out of the room, putting together instruments. She didn't even look at me as she walked by instead heading straight for him. She walked up and took his hand. He pulled her into a hug, and gave her a kiss on the forehead. "Hey," he whispered in her ear.

She smiled. "Hey."

"How's it going? I've missed you."

She laughed. "Three whole days."

"Is that all?"

"I know it feels like a lifetime."

"Definitely."

"I'm going to go say goodbye."

"Absolutely." He let her out of his arms.

She ran over to her senior friends throwing her arms around them. "I can't believe you are leaving me!" She took pictures and talked, dancing about the room, floating from group to group; totally at ease, comfortable in this place that had become her home. She didn't know everyone in the room, but she knew most and they were her chosen family. And in turn most knew her. No matter what group she approached there was someone there to embrace, and laugh with, to make plans of getting together this summer, or to wish best of luck in the future. Some knew her only as Roger's girlfriend, the one the drummers were always teasing to "get a room", but most knew her as the bubbly girl, who was always laughing, giggling, smiling, who always had a kind word, who worked hard and loved that band with her heart and soul. Most knew Drue.

I watched Drue move from group to group. I watched her laugh, and dance, and smile. I wondered if I should ask her to sign my yearbook, she hadn't asked me. I wouldn't even know what to write if she did. We had barely talked in the last two months. She has adjusted to life without me in an effortless act of new friends and a new social circle that Roger's ever climbing drummer status brought. Still I never stopped hoping we'd get back what we once had. I missed her. I missed my best friend.

She snuck off just as soon as Pompom Circumstance was over. She didn't want to miss seeing her sister. So she left the band and hurried over to where she could see the ceremony. She didn't have to wait long.

"And now, presenting your Val Victorian, Stacey Potter!"

Drue clapped and cheered, and her smile went from ear to ear. She was proud of her sister. Proud of all she had accomplished, proud she was up there making the speech. Drue was proud to be the sister of someone who would undoubtedly go on to greatness. Drue knew her sister was capable of anything and everything if she wanted it. She was that smart.

Stacey smiled at the audience. Totally confident, totally calm, as if speaking in front of thousands of people was nothing at all. Drue could never understand that. How thousands of people were the same as talking to a small group to Stacey while for Drue the mere thought made her tremble. But that was Stacey, fearless.

"Thank you," Stacey began....

They pulled into the parking lot and got out. The air was cool and she tugged her sweater around her. He came around and, opening the door, took her hand. The air was crisp and a slight breeze tickled her face. The sun was beginning to set bouncing rays of colour out along the water and extending upon the horizon.

"So you want to walk?" He asked her.

"But you hate walks on the beach," Drue countered softly.

"Well, I'll make an exception just this once."

She smiled. But there was something in the pit of her stomach, something that she couldn't shake. Exceptions were bad, the voice in her head screamed at her, something wasn't right. They began to walk.

She could feel the sand beneath her feet and she wiggled her toes as the sand forced its way into her shoes and under her socks. She looked around, taking a deep breath of air, pure, fresh.

She stopped and began taking off her shoes. "Come in with me," she said, rolling up her pants. She looked up at him, half expecting him to say no.

The look on his face was incredulous, but then he smiled. "Ok."

She smiled back. Together they left their shoes and walked into the surf. As their toes felt the first kisses of the water, she jumped back. "It's cold."

"Oh come on," he said pulling her forward.

Her pants slipped down and were quickly soaked. She tried to roll them up, but to no avail and at last she gave up and let them be. He took her hands and pulled her to him. He wrapped his arms around her and there, with the sun setting on the horizon, the breeze blowing her hair away from her face, the waves gently crashing against their ankles, he kissed her. She closed her eyes taking in the whole moment, for this was heaven. She knew it. It was a movie, it was a photograph, and it was perfect.

And as he took her by the hand and they began to walk back to the car, she knew it was the start of the end. She wouldn't admit it, not even to herself, but she knew. Somewhere deep inside her that little voice was telling her that nothing this perfect could last. They had gone as far as they could go together, it could not be more and thus the end was inevitable. The sunset began to fade and she held onto Roger's hand with all her might fighting the tears that pierced her eyes. She loved this boy. She loved him more than anything in the world, and yet she knew she was losing him. She didn't know why or even how, just that it was there. Maybe not tomorrow, maybe not next month, but they would not make it through the summer. No matter how much she loved him, he was going to leave her.

16

July 2nd

Mary,

Happy Summer! Almost July 4th. Time is flying. Everything is changing so fast. It scares me. It scares me to sit in Stacey's room while she packs for college. Or to sit with Roger, and know that somehow we are growing apart. I love him so much. He's the most important person in my life. He is my best friend, my confident, my saviour. He makes me laugh. He makes everything seem easier somehow. I don't know how I would function without him. And yet, yet I feel like I can't change. Like I have to stay that person he fell in love with so he'll continue to love me. And life is moving, it's always moving. Life is change. And that scares me. I hate change. I hate growing up. Why can't everything just stay the same?

- Drue.

They sat on the edge of the pier. Her feet dangled over the

side and she swung them as she sat, enjoying the slight whooshing sound they made in the calm air. It was beautiful, a clear summer evening. She stole a glance at Roger and saw him staring off into the distance intently. She could tell something was wrong, but she knew Roger would tell her in time. She no longer needed to insist that he tell her, because she knew he would, when he was ready. She liked that. She knew Roger didn't talk to many people, but he talked to her, and she was glad. She liked that they could sit comfortably in silence together and stare out at the ocean. She liked it here, the cool air on her bare skin, the smell of salt that hung in the air, and she liked that beside her sat someone whom she loved. Still something was wrong, and Drue wondered when Roger would tell her what it was that was making him run his hand through his hair, and making the vain on his forehead appear every few moments as he frowned into the distance.

When the sun was no longer visible against the horizon, Drue picked herself up and dusted the sand from her jeans. She held a hand out to Roger, who took it and pulled himself up as well. Hand in hand they walked back to his car.

On the drive back to her house he said it, "I think we don't talk enough."

She looked over at him confused. "What do you mean?"

"Well we are in silence a lot, it feels awkward."

Her heart sank, a feeling of dread crept over her, but she tried to push it aside. "I think our silence is nice. It means we are comfortable with each other." Where was this going? Her mind raced.

"I just think we used to have more to talk about, that's all."

"But we still talk. And when we don't, I take it as a sign that we are comfortable enough with each other to sit in silence. That means something, a good something." Why do I feel like I'm pleading with him? She wondered. Why does this feel so important?

Then they reached her house. "You are right," he said dismissively. "It's no big deal. Night, I love you Drue."

"Night Roger." She climbed out of the car deflated.

"Hey Drue?" He called after her, she turned, "it's going to be okay."

She smiled, trying to believe him. "I know. Love you too." Then she walked into the house.

"Are you scared?" Drue asked as she sat on the couch watching her sister sort through her clothes.

"No, not really. I think it will be exciting." Stacey held up her homecoming dress, "you think I'll need this?"

Drue shrugged. "Doubt it, but how would I know? Maybe they have lots of formals in college."

"Yeah, I better take it," Stacey said looking at the two piles on the floor and throwing the dress into the ever-growing 'to pack' pile.

"So how'd things go with James?"

Stacey picked up another shirt and, pulling it over her head, turned to look in the mirror. "Um, actually quite smoothly, we're going to remain friends and everything, and it's not like we could stay together with an entire continent between us."

"Are you going to miss him?"

Stacey pulled off the shirt and turned to look at her little sister. "Of course. But there's email, and the phone" She threw the shirt into the discard pile. "I think it will be good for us."

Drue nodded. She didn't understand how her sister could be so calm about leaving the guy she had been dating for the last two years. How could a break up be such a rational, calm, thought out event? It was awe inspiring.

"So what do you think?" Stacey asked giving a spin in yet another outfit.

Drue nodded approvingly, "I like the top, ditch the skirt."

Stacey followed her sister's advice tossing the outfit in the two piles respectively. "So you think you might be joining me at Stanford in two years?" She said winking at her sister. "'Cause you know, they give you extra points on your application if you have a sibling already there." Stacey grinned.

Drue laughed. "Sorry, Stace, extra points or not there is no way I'm smart enough to get into Stanford."

"You know that's not true, you are just as smart as I am."

"Yeah, that's exactly why I'm 25th in class rank instead of fighting for 1st." Drue grinned. "It's okay, I'll let you be the brains of the family."

"Great, that means you get to be the good looks of the family, right?" Stacey said, returning the grin as she went to the closet in search of more clothes.

"Yeah, that must be it, especially as we look exactly alike." Drue said to her sister's retreating back.

"Nah, you're more exotic looking," Stacey called from the closet.

"But you are thinner."

"You're taller."

"Your lip doesn't curl up when you smile."

"Your hair's not as frizzy."

"It's also not as thick," her sister walked out of the closet.

Drue erupted in giggles, "Stacey what is that?"

"It's my leotard!"

"But ...it's....full...body...." Drue said amidst her laughter, "and...hot...pink!"

"So you don't think I should take it, huh?" Stacey asked doing a graceful peroet in the middle of the room.

Drue gave a shake of her head. "No, " she said in a small voice trying to hold back the laughter.

Her sister sighed. "Alright."

"Girls! Dinner!"

Both girls turned to look at the clock.

"Doesn't it seem early for dinner? "Stacey asked.

Drue just shrugged helplessly. Leaving her sister to change, Drue extracted herself from the couch as she responded to the summons of dinner.

"Isn't it a bit early for dinner?" She asked as she entered the kitchen.

"Yes, but Mom has a lecture at six thirty." Her dad answered as he took the juice from the fridge.

"Drue, would you mind setting the table?"

"Sure." She began taking cutlery from the drawer, "couldn't we eat after Mom left?"

"You could," Drue's mom interjected from where she stood by the stove, "but my first born is leaving in a month and a half and I don't want to miss a single family dinner." Just then Stacey walked in and her mom took her in a hug as she walked past.

"Riiight," Drue said as she turned toward the dinning room, "five o' clock dinners here we come."

"So what do you think you're going to do tonight?" Her friend asked. They stood in the parking lot of the church waiting to be picked up. The youth group meeting had gotten out early which left a full Sunday night ahead with no plans.

"Dunno" Drue said, and then added, as the idea occurred to her, "maybe I'll call Roger. Maybe we can go to a movie or something." She hadn't seen him since practice on Thursday and she missed him. It was weird without seeing him every day at school. She picked up her cell phone and called him, he wasn't there. Her friend raised her eyebrows. "He wasn't there." Drue said with a shrug of her shoulders.

"Well you can always try again later."

"Yeah," Drue agreed a little sad, "he's probably just out."

"So how are you two?" She asked

"We're fine," Drue answered briefly. "And what of you, any new boys?"

Her friend smiled. "Well there is this boy in my biology class……"

After her friend was picked up Drue sat down and decided to try Roger again. He still wasn't there. That was weird.

She went over to his house the next day.

"What are you doing here?" he asked.

"Just thought I'd stop by to say hi."

"Oh, well come in. What's up?"

Drue walked in. They sat in the living room, and when Drue sat on the couch Roger sat across from her, that felt weird. She shrugged. "Nothing, just wanted to see how you were. It's been awhile."

"So why'd you call so many times last night?"

"I don't know. I just wanted to see you, go to a movie or something."

"But my mom said you called like four times."

"Well you weren't home. I thought maybe you'd get in." She looked at him, was he angry? She couldn't tell.

"Well anyway, so now you are here, what do you want to do?"

"I don't know. How are you? How's life? I feel like it has been forever."

"Yeah I guess I've just been kind of busy."

"With what?" She asked curiously.

"Aw, just stuff."

"Alriiiight," Drue said slowly, "so what should we do?"

"I don't know. We don't have much time. I'm having dinner in a like half an hour."

"Oh." Pause. His tone wasn't unkind, his words not particularly hurtful and yet Drue felt something crumble within her. Something was very wrong. "Well then, maybe I should just leave." She got up.

"Alright," he got up. "Drue." He tried to give her a hug, but she pulled away. "Drue, it's going to be okay" he told her, "I love you, everything will work out."

But she pulled away. She was hurt, and embarrassed, upset that she let him get to her, upset she cared so much, upset that she had come over and been such a nag. So she pulled away and left.

She didn't know that would be the last time he would try to hug her, or the last time she would hear those words from him. She didn't know that was the end. Somewhere deep down she did, but on the surface she believed him. She believed he loved her, and that everything would be okay.

But then he didn't call or talk to her for a week. Even at band, he was only polite, not saying goodbye when he left, or giving her a hug when he saw her. She should have known then.

She didn't tell anyone. She didn't let her fears show, not even to me.

So when I received a call one evening in July I didn't really listen. It was her and she said "hi" and then paused. It was awkward and difficult, and I was on my way out. When I told her that, she said, "Ok" and hung up. I didn't know she was calling because he had broken up with her.

She hung up the phone then. She went into her sister's room and crawled into the bed and waited. At last Stacey got home. She held her baby sister tightly as she cried. She tried to reassure Drue, and when that didn't work she just held her and told her it would be okay. Her arms felt safe, the same embrace that earlier in the year had made the tears disappear, but this time it wasn't enough, she wasn't enough, Drue was dead inside. There were tears that never stopped, and there was pain that she had never felt before, and she didn't know what to do. Because she didn't know how to fight this kind of pain. So she smiled, and at last told Stacey thanks and goodnight. Then she climbed out of bed and back to her own room. There she sat on her bed and cried. Totally alone for she had nowhere else to go.

And still I knew nothing. I didn't know then how Roger had come over that day, and sat on her bed and told her his life was too complicated right now, that she just didn't fit in anymore, that he wanted to love her, but just didn't. I didn't know how she watched him leave unable to breathe for the tears that tore through her, or how he ran the short distance down her driveway escaping as quickly as he could from the look of pain so clearly written on her face. And I didn't know how for the next week she slept on the couch because she couldn't look at that bed. Instead, I was sitting at home that night, bored because nothing good was on TV, unaware that in my best friend's world the sky had just caved in upon her and nothing was ever to be the same again.

JUNIOR YEAR: Broken

"When faced with the unthinkable, one chooses the merely impossible."
- 'The Beekeeper's Apprentice', Laurie R. King

PRESENT DAY: AUGUST

Drue is lying on her back, her face turned upward taking in the warmth of the summer sun. She turns herself over to look at me and explain, "Of my two best friends, one was bulimic, the other is currently battling anorexia, you suffered depression, my sister is OCD, and my mom has her own issues. It should have been a given that I would be screwed up somehow."

"But you didn't know all that then," I counter.

"No, then I was just a 16 year old girl who found the world falling down around her. I didn't know that it was probably inevitable anyway."

"But Drue, you led the perfect life. "

"Thus the inevitability. Don't you see Chris? Eventually I was going to have to learn that life wasn't perfect. That relationships aren't perfect. That people aren't perfect. Eventually the world was going to fall."

I just shrug. "I dunno, I like to believe maybe you could have been saved."

She smiles. "Me too Chris, me too." She rolls back over onto her back and closes her eyes.

17

July 20th

He left. Just like that. He left. I can't breathe.

– Drue.

Rain....the tears of the gods. That's what they say, right? Well it rained the day he left her; a summer storm. "Amazing," people said. The first in years to hit our quaint little California town. They didn't know the gods were crying for her. They didn't know that he left that day, saying that he "wanted to love her, but just didn't anymore." They didn't know that with him she lost everything. It seemed that after he left it didn't matter how great her parents were or how much her friends tried to help, she just didn't see them anymore. To her all she saw was the rain.....

Drue raised her hand against the glass as they drove away. Her sister waved back in return as she stood on the front steps of the dorms. A tear rolled down Drue's cheek. Then they turned out of the parking lot and Stacey became lost amongst the trees that lined the street. Drue turned back around in her seat.

"Well now I guess it's just you," Drue's mom said turning around and patting her daughter on the knees.

Drue forced a smile. Then she put her head phones on and lay her head against the window hoping for sleep.

Drue's sister was the smartest person either of us ever knew and so it felt only natural that she got into one of the most prestigious universities in the world. But it meant Drue's sister was now going to be five hours away and it meant Drue would be on her own. All her life Drue had felt most special because she was her sister's sister. She knew who she was because she was a baby Potter. She looked forward to those times after school when she would sit in her sister's room and listen to her tell stories of her exciting life. Drue lived for her sister. When they were little Drue's sister was the movie star and Drue the adoring fan, it was the part she played well. She would run into her sister's room, demanding her autograph, wanting just a glimpse of the magnificence that was her. So when Drue's sister left, she took with her that magnificence. She left Drue without someone to be the shadow of; she left Drue alone in the spotlight. It was a place Drue had never been nor wanted to be. She didn't even know where to begin. The idea alone scared her.

She told his best friend. She assumed he would know, and so when he looked at her critically and asked, "Drue is everything okay?" She was almost bewildered.

"Don't you know?"

"Know what?" He asked confused. Over the past year he and Drue had become friends and though her friendship would never rival Roger's, he considered himself fairly up to date on Drue's life.

"That Roger broke up with me?"

His eye's widened. "He did what?"

"I thought you knew."

"The bastard! Is he crazy? No, of course I didn't know. I'm so sorry. You want me to beat him up for you?"

Drue just laughed. "No, it's ok. Thanks though, for the thought."

It became a common offer as she told people about the break-up. She would always just laugh and thank them kindly for the thought, but she was fine. People didn't understand how the perfect couple had broken up and when they asked, she didn't know what to tell them, because, she didn't know either.

18

September 15th

Dear Espera,

Since you see the world through your eyes, and only your eyes, then when you change does the world change? Can other people see the changes that were caused by your different viewing of the world? What then is the world really like? For we all see it differently so how do we know what's real? We think we all see the same thing, because we talk about it, but couldn't it be utterly different yet merely thought to be the same? Like if someone else's green was different from mine- we both call it green and thus we assume we are talking about the same thing - but how do we know for sure? I guess that's what cameras are for. I don't know. It seems the world must be physically different since everything else has changed.- but do other people see those changes? After all their lives haven't just been altered. Maybe they do change but no one notices.
– Drue Potter

PS- I shall name you Espera. I seem to be lacking in hope right now. So perhaps you can be my hope for me.

Drue had this amazing belief that if you were a good person life would be good to you. It never occurred to her that sometimes shit happens. That sometimes life doesn't go as planned, that there are lessons to be learned, pain makes us stronger, and life isn't always perfect. When she lost him, she was, for the first time in her life, forced to realize these truths. She began to understand the world I had been living in for the last year. The thing was, Drue was never meant for this world. She was meant to stay in her bubble, where everyone loved her, took care of her, and never hurt her. She was meant to stay where there were smiles, hugs, and kind words.

She began to reach out and craw into the corner of depression where I had been alone for the last year. As glad as I was for the company, I didn't want her to share it with me. I wanted Drue to be the smiling, giggling girl she had been since I'd met her. The girl Roger made her. I knew she still loved him, I saw it in her whole face. I saw it in the way she looked at him, the way she cringed when he flirted with other girls, the way she had to look away when he was having too much fun, or was too happy.

I knew the looks because I had been there. I had watched her and him with those same looks and pain behind them. The difference was that I had grown accustomed to these feelings, the gnawing that incessantly pulls at your heart, the tears that are always threatening, the hole in the pit of your stomach that you can't seem to fill, I had grown accustomed to these things and learned to deal with them as part of life, but Drue hadn't. She had never been taught that people could hurt you. No one had just left her life suddenly one day; she had never lost anyone, or experienced real pain. No one had ever hated Drue or avoided her, or not met her eyes. She had never had her best friend walk by without seeing her. The realization that all of a sudden people you think are always going to be there go away and don't come back, well for Drue, that knowledge broke her.

That was also the week her parents began fighting. They never yelled, they never said hurtful words about one another; they just didn't speak to each other. When they did speak it was polite conversations, and it made Drue nervous. It left her feeling always on edge, as if she were walking on an ice covered lake, and one wrong step might start a crack that would end up shattering the ice and throwing her into the freezing water below. She didn't know what would happen then, but it couldn't be good.

The bell rang. Drue hurriedly packed her bag and pushed her way to the door. She proceeded to sweep past the herds of students as she made her way to the parking lot. She didn't look to either side, careful not to catch anyone's eye. She cared only about making it to her car, which she did, throwing her bag on the seat beside her. She drove the short distance to the park that sat beside the school holding her breath all the while. Only when she was in the safety of the trees did she allow herself to breath out fully, an act that started the predictable flood of tears. Uncontrollable sobs that echoed through her and escaped so violently that she shook as she leaned over the steering wheel trying to steady herself.

Eventually the tears slowed, the shaking stopped and Drue was left with only a dull head ache. She breathed in deeply. The day was over, she had survived. She had smiled, and gone to class. She had seen him, walked past him, and she hadn't broken down. She had made it through the day, and now like every other day so far this year she sat and recovered from it. She hated this part of the day. The uncontrollable tears that she was too weak to fight against.

Everyone expected her to be better by now, even she thought that surely after three months the pain would have lessened, and yet every afternoon she found herself here, beneath the trees crying. She hated herself for not being stronger. She hated herself for not being able to fight this thing that she knew was going to happen. How could she not have been better prepared? She had always thought herself capable of handling anything, and yet now here she was utterly helpless to deal with this thing that was only a minor heartache.

Those tears became her enemy. Tears that only magnified an already incessant feeling of helplessness. Drue hated that feeling. She was not helpless. She would fight this. She would find some way to fight those tears, to get rid of them. Then one day, she did.

19

October 19th

Dear Espera,

I miss Roger. It always comes back to him. Freshman year we became friends in Vegas and were flirting by Halloween, last year he asked me out in Las Vegas and we were head over heels for each other by Halloween. It's just not the same this year. I don't want to start from ground zero with some new guy. Homecoming was hard. Sitting home while I knew Roger was out with some girl was hard. I miss being special in his eyes, I miss him wanting to be my friend. Maybe that's asking lot. Mom and Dad say he's handling it badly - that he always did, I think they are just mad 'cause they see how much I still hurt. I don't think he's done anything so particularly wrong. He just doesn't care anymore. Can I blame him for that? G'night.

Love Drue Potter

PS- It would be Roger and my one year anniversary today.

She picked up the razor and looked at it critically. Yes, it looked sharp enough. She held it to her skin, lightly, feeling the tickling sensation of metal on skin. I wonder if a used razor could give me some kind of disease, she thought idly. Then quickly, lightly, in one swift motion, she moved the blade across her skin. It was a small cut, not more than two inches long. She looked at it numbly for a long moment. She'd done it, actually acted on the desire that had been growing inside her for so long. Part of her was exhilarated, looking at the new line that lay on her leg, however; another part of her was disappointed, there was no blood. She must not have cut deep enough. With a small breath she quickly made a slightly deeper cut next to the first. It was lopsided and before she had time to think she had made a third and fourth cut. It was then that she saw the blood, a thin line coming to the surface displaying the odd contortion of lines that lay near her ankle. Then the pain came, a dull ach, but one that she relished in. This kind of pain she could handle. She knew how to be strong against this kind of pain. She fingered the scars gingerly, delighted in her little secret.

She had known she needed help for weeks, months even, but when none was offered she resorted to her own means. And it had worked, despite the awful knot that lay in her stomach, she felt better. Calm, for the first time in months.

She took a deep breath; everything was going to be okay.

She pulled her pants back down over the cuts and got up to resume her homework. After all, it was still just like any other night and she had homework to do.

I can't remember how she told me. I only remember it was in passing, an online conversation or slipped into a night-time chat as if it was the most natural thing in the world. But it wasn't natural, and it wasn't normal and the statement resonated deep in me, shaking the ground I had been standing on. This giggly, happy girl was cutting. I had known she was broken just not the extent of it. And I was powerless to save her. I knew that too.

There wasn't anything I could do or say. Even if such a brilliant statement existed I was in the same corner, and I couldn't see a way out for either of us. So I stood by and had to watch as she broke unable to help her, unable to save her.

She began to cut regularly. It became part of her routine. Like putting on makeup she would do it on those days that were important, that she really needed God's help. It was her way of making sure God was looking out for her that day, insuring that things went okay. She knew it was wrong, and she tried to convince herself that cutting and how good her day went were unrelated, but she couldn't. She truly believed that the days when she cut turned out better. Often on days when she would have to be near him for extended periods of time she would cut, just to make sure everything would go okay. So she cut almost every weekend just before we boarded the buses for competitions, and she cut some days before school just to make sure band went well that day, or that she'd do okay on her test, or that someone would be there to eat lunch with. Whatever the scary part of her life, Drue would conquer it through cutting.

"How was school?" Her mom asked that night at dinner as she poured herself a glass of wine.

Drue shrugged. "Fine," she answered.

"Anything exciting happening?" Her dad asked.

Drue shook her head. "Nope."

"Well…." Her mom let the statement trail off. They ate in silence.

Drue wished her sister was there. Stacey always had a way of filling dinner time conversation. There was always some new drama in Stacey's life, or dilemma to be brought to the attention of the family. She was always doing things, winning awards, or going places. Drue wouldn't even know where to begin with such stories. Her days were all the same, blending together like the grains of sand on the beach, indistinguishable one from the other, and only recognizable if one took out the magnify glass. So most nights dinnertime passed in silence, Drue watching as her mother would go through half a bottle of wine and merely push her food around on her plate. Drue wondered if her parents would allow her to do the same. Then at least maybe she wouldn't eat so much, and maybe there was something to this drinking thing. Drue had never tried it, but maybe at some point she ought to.

Anything to numb the pain.

20

October 24th

Dear *Espera,*

I always thought the purpose of this life was to love, but then after you have loved and lost what is the point anymore? To love again? Why would I want to love again? What is fate's plan for me now that I have completed all I know? I hate not knowing… that is the scariest part, that I no longer know what the point of life is, because then the question becomes: why am I living life at all?

- Drue

He had moved on. He had gotten his life together, and moved on. He began to date a new girl. One that was nothing like Drue. She watched their relationship progress. She was on the bus when he asked the girl out. *Armageddon* was playing on the TV screens overhead and Drue looked back to where Roger was sitting, just to see if he also was thinking of her; to see if he also remembered. He was kissing the girl beside him.

Drue felt the floor drop out from under her. Her head swam and she couldn't steady herself. The world around her became a blur and the only thing she felt was a gnawing in her stomach, a doubling over of pain that she couldn't control. And so she curled up in a little ball and cried.

I was sitting across from her. I watched in horror as she began to sob. I looked back at him, glaring at him, wondering how he could be so cruel. But I knew it was not cruelty that caused him to hurt her, only ignorance. He just didn't know better. I sighed wondering what I should do.

"Go to her. Comfort her," the voice was just barely audible over the bus sounds. I looked at the girl sitting next to me; she nodded toward Drue. "Forgive her. Let last year be the past. She needs you now."

I watched Drue, curled up on her seat. She sat alone now, for after sitting with Roger for two years, she had no one else. And as she sat there hugging her knees to her chest she looked so very young; young, afraid and alone. No past hurt was worth making her suffer like that. But that was not what stopped me. I had forgiven Drue long ago, put last year behind me and accepted her back as my confidant and friend. But what stopped me now was fear. Her pain scared me, for I did not know that there was anything I could do. I was scared she would reject my support, which would be so much worse then not offering it in the first place.

The girl beside me gave me a small push. "Go," she breathed into my ear. I got up and went across the isle. I took Drue's hand. She looked at me briefly, gave me a half hearted smile before turning away from me. But she kept my hand in hers and did not try to withdraw it. I sat staring at the seat in front of me, she stared out the window. Neither of us said a word. Anything I said would be inadequate and anything she said would start her crying again, so instead we just sat.

Soon her breathing returned to normal, and I felt her gain control. Then something else happened. As she stopped crying, her desperation turned to energy, sitting still became intolerable.

She began to bounce her legs and squirm in her seat. When we arrived at our destination she let go of my hand without a word. She left the bus without so much as a glance in my direction. She dropped her bag on the gym floor where we would be sleeping that night and then headed toward the stairwell.

Up and down, up and down the stairs she ran. Her music played through her head phones and she threw her whole effort into focusing on each stair as she ascended and then descended. The concrete was cold on her bare feet and she was going at such speeds that she had to steady herself on the railing as she rounded the turn so that she wouldn't fall. Her lungs began to hurt, and her breathing became uneven, but she didn't stop. She couldn't stop. If she stopped the tears would come. She tried it once. Stopping at the top of the stairs to catch her breath, but the sobs instantly threaten and the pain in her stomach became unbearable so she started to move again, faster, quicker, to stop the crying. Crying was weak, and she wasn't weak.

At the bottom of the stairs stood the girl. Roger's new girlfriend. She watched Drue running the stairs like a madwoman. "Drue.... listen… Can I talk to you for a minute…"

Drue slowed, looking at the girl. She tried to make her mind focus, tried to bring herself into the present moment, but then the sobs began to threaten. She wouldn't let this girl see her cry, she couldn't. She shook her head. "Is it okay if I just do my stairs right now?"

The girl looked at her and nodded. "Yeah…." Drue returned to her running and the girl stood there for a minute watching, before she left.

Drue watched as the girl stood there, and let out a sign of relief when she left. Drue wouldn't let her see how much she was hurting, at least not just yet, not now.

She continued her running, up and down, up and down. A few minutes later another figure appeared at the bottom of the stairs. This one, though not ideal, was welcome. Drue slowed, "hey."

"Hey," I replied. "How are you doing?"

"Fine I guess," she answered unconvincingly as she slowed to talk to me. She didn't stop completely, but she resumed at a normal pace so that I might walk beside her as she made her ascent.

I could see the tears on her flushed cheeks. She had tied her hair back into a loose ponytail but parts had escaped the rubber band and she now took the time to tuck them back in.

"I'm sorry," I said helplessly. I knew how much she was hurting, and all I could come up with to say was I'm sorry!

She rewarded me with a weak smile. "It's not your fault."

" I know, but I feel bad. Is there anything I can do?"

"I'll be fine, don't worry about it," she answered in her normal dismissal of all pain as if the present would just be made to go away with those simple words.

"I know you will," I responded as I always did, because, what else was there to say?

She stopped and sat down at the top of the stairs. I sat beside her. She stared at her hands. "I just hurt," silence, "I'm just so freakin' mad! "She got up and went down the stairs. "I want to kill myself. I hurt so bad," she looked back to where I still sat above her and added, "I won't really. I'm not brave enough for it. Though you should probably take this razor away from me." But I didn't take the razor from her. She began to run again. I watched until at last, helplessly, I left.

Drue sat down. She reached into her pocket and took out the razor that was there; the razor she had put there earlier that evening. She looked at it for a long moment, running it over her finger gingerly. Then she pulled up her pant leg and made a hard cut. She put all her anger in that cut, all her pain, and guilt, and sadness. And with it, some of the pain disappeared. She made another mark across it; making a perfect X. This, she told herself, is to remind me of this night. By the time this scar disappears I will be over it. I will have forgotten.

The cut bled deeply. She went to the bathroom to wash the blood, and yet there remained stains on her pants that would not disappear.

She returned to the gym which was filled with all her classmates and friends. Everyone was sombre. On a night that they should have been having the time of their lives, everyone talked in whispers. All her friends knew what had happened, knew how she must be hurting. And when she walked back into the room it felt as if all eyes turned to her. She picked up her head. "Smile" she told herself, "don't show your weakness."

But all she could think about that night was what it would be like to slit her wrists, to feel the blood flowing down her arms. The release and freedom from such a deep cut. And then what would happen? She forced herself to think, she was in a room with thirty other people, someone would notice. They'd have to wrap up her arms in bandages, take her to the hospital. Then what? Her parents. Her parents would find out. And because of her parents, Drue didn't move to find her razor. She didn't touch her razor to her skin, and she forced herself to lie in bed silently until at last, she fell asleep. By the morning the whole thing was a dream. Except for the scar, that would remain for some time yet.

"It will make you stronger."

I felt more than saw her wince at the remark.

To her friend Drue only smiled. "Yes, I know."

But as her friend left she turned to me with a pained expression on her face. "Why? Why do I have to be stronger?" The remark was more of a plea then a question so I said nothing. "Why does everyone say that, like its such a good thing?" She continued, "I don't want to be stronger. I'm tired of being stronger, of learning my lessons, of growing up. All I want is to be happy again." Her voice was almost a whisper and as she finished a tear rolled down her cheek and she looked at me searching for something, but what? An answer? Reassurance? What could I give her to make it better? I couldn't get him back for her.

I would have. I would have taken back all my own pain to relieve her of her own. But I couldn't. So I patted her on the shoulder and tried to sound convincing as I said the empty words, "it's going to be okay."

She gave me a half smile and shook her head. "No, no it's not.

Not anymore. It's not going to be okay." And with that she got up and left.

I watched her go, wondering how, now that I had my best friend back at last, I could help her become the person she once had been.

Her sister called. She had a new boyfriend. She was in love and everything was amazing. Drue's sister was one of those people who lived in a world that was always either perfect or falling apart. Drue would return home from school on some days to find her parents pacing the kitchen nervously. Stacey had called. She had been in tears. She had said something terrible had happened, and now she couldn't be reached. Did Drue know what it could be? They hoped it wasn't anything too serious, but then Stacey had sounded very upset.

Later in the night Stacey would call back, all laughter and smiles. The emergency had been fixed, it was just a bad grade on a test, but she had talked to her professor, oh and by the way this boy had asked her out. So really, things were okay after all. Her parents would talk to her sister and Drue would hang up the phone silently, hoping that perhaps they wouldn't notice that she wasn't listening, that she couldn't listen. How could she hear about how perfect her sister's life was? How could she listen to the excitement of a new school, new boys and new friends? How could she take joy in the life that she wasn't allowed to be a part of? Her sister was moving on, she was growing up, and Drue was being left behind. She wouldn't let Stacey know how much that hurt, how much Drue missed her big sister, her role model, her idol and the person that she strove to emulate more than anyone in the world. Drue wouldn't let her sister know any of these things, and so when she began to miss Stacey too much Drue would hang up the phone silently, the tears rolling down her cheeks, and she would hug her knees to her chest concentrating on taking deep breaths. Slowly, carefully, she would regain control. Then she would go to the bathroom, wash her face and kiss her parents goodnight, absently, while they were still on the phone so they wouldn't notice her red eyes.

Then she would climb into bed. Her prayers were short: "bless everyone and let them be good. Let me be good and let Stacey be happy at Stanford. Please let everyone's dreams come true. Please let my dreams come true." The problem was she didn't even know what her dreams were anymore. What did she want? She wanted to be whole again, she wanted things to go back to the way they were; she wanted not to be sad anymore. But she wasn't sure how to get that. The loneliness was too great, and the tears would come, and she would send all her love to her sister who was so far away, and hope that she was doing well. Drue hoped that her sister would never have to go through what Drue felt now, that maybe if she suffered enough, Stacey would never have too. Maybe God would be satisfied with just one of them learning the lesson of a broken heart, so Stacey could be spared. Drue wished that for her sister.

She looked down and her heart skipped a beat, 142 lbs. She had never weighted so much in her life, it had to be wrong, that was the only possible explanation; the scale had to be broken. She got off and back on. One hundred and forty lbs, it was still there. Drue stood frozen as the number blinked up at her. Well, she had to stop eating, that was the only solution. Drue walked into her room and took out the razor from her purse. She made one cut, a small and clean line across the top of her hand, just as a reminder. Like tying a string around her finger it would be her reminder: eat healthy, or don't eat.

21

December 17th

Dear *Espera,*

I miss Stacey. I miss having someone else around. The house is so quiet without her. No music from her room, no singing from the shower. No absurd knocking communication system through the wall that I never understood. No one to get hugs from after a long day at school. No one to commiserate with when Mom and Dad are in a bad mood. No one to tell me stories so I can forget my own. No one to remind me who I am. It's hard work to figure that out on my own. I don't think I'm doing a very good job.

– Drue

PS- She'll be home soon for the holidays. That will be real nice. It's been a long time.

I watched Drue. She sat staring at the blackboard, but she wasn't paying attention. Her pen moved across the paper writing the notes on the board, but her eyes weren't watching what she was writing, instead they stared off into the distance, distracted. She didn't smile as much as she used to, she rarely laughed. And when she spoke in class, though still with the same insight and poise, there was no joy in her voice, there was no teasing, no fun. She swore now.

I looked across the room to where Roger sat. He too was watching Drue. I wondered what he was thinking, if he knew he had caused this change in her. Yes, I decided looking at him, he knew. He just didn't see a way of helping without giving up his own happiness, something he wasn't willing to do. So he would continue to flirt and date other girls. I don't think he did it maliciously, just ignorantly. He didn't know the other things going on in her life, how could he? So he had no way of knowing how much she needed him right now and thus how much his absence hurt her.

Roger looked back to the board. I looked back at Drue. She had not noticed. Her eyes were blank. She brushed a wisp of hair out of her face. Then the bell rang.

Her parents talked behind closed doors now. She would lie in bed at night praying for sleep as their murmurings continued long into the night and continued when she awoke in the morning. Sometimes there was crying. These were the nights Drue hated most. She began to wear headphones to bed trying to block out the sobs, the pain of her parents. Pain that she didn't know, nor wanted to know the cause of. She wanted to scream at them on those nights, slap them and yell and ask if their pain was as great as hers. Ask if they even noticed her anymore, or if their pain took that knowledge away from them. But she wouldn't cry, she wouldn't reach for her razor, instead she grew hard, her heart cold. Her stomach became a knot and she would throw herself into the music that pulsed through her ears. Her music became her solace, her escape, her savour.

In the morning her parent's door would still be closed. There was no longer anyone up to make her breakfast, or to pack her a lunch. There was no one there to say goodbye, or to wish her a good day. Drue would leave for school alone, having never seen her parents despite being able to hear them through closed doors. She wondered sometimes if her parents ever missed her, even a little bit. If they noticed that they were losing their daughter. Drue noticed, and she missed them very much.

It was fourth period when we got our PSAT scores back. Drue sat in the back of the room holding the small slip of paper in her hand willing it to say something good. Then she took a deep breath and opened it. Her heart sank. It wasn't a bad number, but it was not going to get her a national merit scholarship, hell she'd be lucky if it'd get her into a good school. She looked at her hands, they had begun to shake, and the room was beginning to feel a little stifling. Oh God, she thought numbly, she knew what this meant.

I watched Drue open her envelope. My own still sat on my desk in front of me. I didn't see much point in opening the thing. It didn't matter anyway. My hopes for college were limited at best. SAT scores didn't matter much, PSAT scores even less. However, I knew that wasn't the case for Drue. I knew that no matter how much she tried to pretend otherwise she would always strive to be like her sister, and that meant doing well on her PSATs.

Drue's face was blank as she looked at the paper. But then I saw her glance at her hands, I saw her look around the room; I saw her eyes go to the clock. I knew the warning signs by now and so was not surprised when a moment later she got up and slipped out of the door. I followed.

"Drue." She turned, her eyes were blank. "You okay? How'd you do?"

She shook her head. "Fine, I did fine," she said trying to mask her wavering voice. Then she turned and continued to walk away. I ran to catch up.

"Hey wait up. You sure you're okay? Where're you going?"

"Just the bathroom. Don't worry Chris, I'm fine." By the time we reached the bathroom her eyes were glistening with tears, she wiped them away before pushing the door open. She didn't give me a backward glance.

She slipped inside the door just as her breathing became difficult, before the tears started and the world slid about in a dizzying disorder. She had really thought she'd do better. She knew she wasn't as smart as her sister, but she always believed this was just because she chose not to work as hard, it didn't occur to her that she actually wasn't as smart. But here was the proof, on an aptitude test she just didn't measure up. It was like a blow to the head, the knowledge that she just wasn't that smart. She took out her razor. She carved a dark F into her leg, failure. That's what she was, a failure. She looked at her watch, shit, now she was missing class. She got up and wiped her eyes. She looked in the mirror, could you tell something was wrong? She did her best to dry her eyes; she put a smile on her face. No one would know, people don't like to believe something is wrong, if you give them a smile, they soon forget the tears in your eyes.

When she came out of the bathroom I was waiting for her. "You didn't have to wait," she said upon seeing me. "Now we are both late for class."

I shrugged. "Luckily, I find it bearable to miss fifteen minutes of pre-calc."

She smiled and rolled her eyes. "Come on, let's go."

"You're sure you're okay?" I asked as we walked.

She nodded. "Yeah. Totally. Honest, Chris. God, don't look so worried. No one died; they call them the *practice* SATs for a reason."

I smile. "Hey you don't have to remind me."

"Drue, Chris!"

We turned at the sound of our names.

"Hey wait up!" We stopped. A girl came running to catch up to us. I felt Drue stiffen as she neared. Sandy was Roger's third girlfriend since Drue, and yet this time it was different. Sandy was one of Drue's oldest friends, a girl she had trusted, confided in, vented to. When he started dating this girl it felt like a betrayal unlike the other two. It wasn't about Roger this time, but about the fact that this girl had used Drue to become friends with Roger in the first place. It somehow made having to hear the stories about "Rogie" all the more difficult to bare. And yet somehow, the girl, whether ignorant or vindictive, always found a way to bring up such a story in conversation. This time was to be no different.

"Hey. Where are you two headed?"

"Actually just back to class. We are running a bit late today," Drue said, about to start walking again.

"Great me too. I stayed back to talk to Ms. Morgan," Sandy said referring to our English teacher. She started to walk with us; I heard Drue let out a small sigh of resignation next to me, "I think I might enter my story into the writing contest." Sandy continued. "What do you guys think? Like, I think it was definitely one of the best ones read in class today, no offence Drue, wouldn't you agree?"

Drue smiled to herself. I could almost hear what was going through her head. "As if Ms. Morgan even asked her to read her story." The period before, Ms. Morgan had asked for a few people to read their stories out loud. The volunteers went first, Sandy being one of them, eagerly raising her hand to read her slice of life memoir about her and Roger. Of course she had changed the names, but everyone knew who it was about. And for Drue, though it was one thing to accept that her friend was dating Roger, it was quite another to have to listen to a story about it, to be made aware that they now had what was only a memory to Drue. But the smile that now played across Drue's lips was not in remembrance of the pain that she had felt when she had had to sit and listen to that story, instead it was of the moment after all the volunteers had gone and Ms. Morgan has asked that Drue and another girl in their class read their stories because they were "written remarkably well." Drue's story had been a portrait of her life over the last five months, of cutting and depression. It had not been something she had wanted to share with the rest of the class, whom she hoped would not make the connection between herself and the character in the book, but she had felt a certain level of pride in being chosen.

"I could never write in that style before," Sandy was saying, "I was just inspired I guess." Drue rolled her eyes at me behind Sandy's back. But I could see that behind the laugher Drue was fighting tears. Sandy continued to talk. "But I'm still not sure what to do about the ending? Like do you think I should keep that part about the kiss, or should I not be so explicit?"

Drue closed her eyes for a long moment trying to calm her pounding heart, trying to keep the threatening tears from giving themselves away in her voice. "You know, I think whatever you do will be good."

"Yeah, well it was an amazing night."

Drue smiled. That fake smile that she had learned so well to assure everyone that everything was okay. But all the while she wondered how her friend could not see how every word out of her mouth, every sentence on the page, hurt her.

I picked up my pace. "Come on Drue. We really have to hurry."

"Oh, right. Sorry guys. See you later!" Sandy gave us a wave and turned off down a hallway. Drue looked at me with a look for relief.

We went back to class.

22

February 19th

Dear *Espera,*

I just finished 'American Gods'. It's the story of how all the gods came to America, brought here by immigrants and then forgotten about as time went on. It says the gods are dying because there is no longer human sacrifice. And I realized that this is why God is nicer to me after a cut. He just needs the human sacrifice. He needs human blood spilled in his honour and I am doing that, I am keeping God alive. Realistically I know this isn't true, after all the entire book is fiction, the idea absurd, cutting is bad, God can't condone that. And yet…it just makes too much sense. That would explain why days are better after I cut. And even if it's just the slightest possibility that its true- well then, I alone may be keeping God alive and enabling Him to protect and keep safe all those I love. How can I jeopardize that?

– *Drue*

"What happened?"

Her friend looked at Drue worriedly. They sat on the bleachers outside of the band room. They were suppose to be in sectionals practicing, but Drue and her friend were instead basking in the sunlight, soaking up the warmth and wasting the day away with idle conversation. Drue followed his glance. A long cut ran across her upper shoulder. It was still pink and slightly puckered which marked its freshness and made it stand out against the pale hue of Drue's tank top. Drue just shrugged, "I dunno." Her brow wrinkled, "maybe I scratched it on a tree or something. It doesn't hurt."

"Hmmm," her friend said. And that was all.

Drue made a mental note to not make any more cuts on her shoulder.

Drue sat at the table after dinner telling her parents about the weekend band competition she had just gotten back from. Her mom was sipping tea; her father was in the kitchen cleaning up. Drue was sitting at the table, a glass of water in front of her. The phone rang. Her father picked it up. He turned to Drue's mother, "it's for you."

Drue knew then. She wasn't sure how she knew. Something about the look between her father and mother, something about the tone in her father's voice, the feeling in the pit of her stomach. She just knew. And so as her mother went to the other room to take the phone call Drue held her breath. She tried to act natural, continuing the conversation with her dad, sipping her water, trying to quiet her pounding heart.

Her mother returned. She looked at Drue. "That was Angela's mom."

Drue nodded, smiled, tried to pretend she didn't know what was coming next.

"She says Angela is worried that you might be cutting," pause, "is that true?"

Drue just looked at her mother. She had returned to her seat at the table in front of her tea. Drue's father had come to sit on the other side of Drue. She knew she was trapped. And yet… she just looked at her mother. The voice inside her screamed. Yes, it said, yes, of course it's true, now help me. Drue took a deep breath.

"Because you know that would just kill us if you were," her mother said then.

Drue stopped. She let the breath out slowly, watching her mom. Her mother's hands were clenched together on her lap, her eyes held a look of pain Drue had never seen before. Drue knew her mom was right, the truth would kill her. So Drue just smiled and shook her head. "No. I'm not. Of course I'm not". She looked her mother in the eye, lying to her for the first time in sixteen years.

Her mother let out her breath, "oh good. Then why do you think Angela thought you were?"

Drue shrugged. "Don't know. The other day we were discussing Chris' depression and I said I understood what he was going through. Maybe it's from that. I meant the depression and stuff, but maybe they assumed something about cutting. I'm sure it's just a misunderstanding."

Her mother nodded. "I can understand the urge to cut," she said thoughtfully, "it centres you back to your body. It's why I rub my legs when I get upset."

Drue only nodded. She wondered how long she would have to stay there. How long would seem natural before she could escape to her room. The air had become stifling, and she was finding it difficult to breathe. She heard herself steering the conversation away from the topic back to the competition of the weekend before. She listened from a far off place as she continued her stories. She wondered if her parents could hear her heart beating wildly, or see how her hands shook. After what felt like an eternity, she at last excused herself. She nearly ran the short distance to her room, throwing herself on to her bed and breathing deeply. Exhausted she lay there for a long time just collecting her thoughts. How was she ever going to make it through this?

Her parents never again mentioned the conversation to Drue, but from that night on they watched their daughter a little more carefully. Was that a new cut on her leg? Or had it been there last week? Could it just be a scratch from a tree branch? What about the one on her arm? Surely that could be from their hike the weekend before, right?

I waited at her car. I twirled the flowers around in my hand. It was awkward holding flowers in a school parking lot. But there I was. It had been a particularly bad competition. Roger had just broken up with his girlfriend and had made a point of acting single again. He flirted, made stupid jokes and teased the freshman. Everyone loved him, it was impossible not to enjoy his irrepressible good humour, his quick wit, his ability to make a fool of himself for a laugh. But it killed her. As much as she tried to keep smiling, there were times when it became impossible and I would see her just walk away. Friends were hard to find now, for if sides had to be chosen all would go with him. Many of the girls hated her simply because she was Roger's ex. Whether out of jealousy, anger, or genuine dislike, for the first time in her life Drue was confronted by girls who flat out hated her. Not for anything she did or could apologize for, but simply for being her.

At last she appeared. She was walking from the bathroom and I watched as she casually ran the back of her hand across her jeans. I didn't have to look to know this meant she had a new cut there. The back of her hand was often where Drue cut on band weekends, it was a place she could cut on the bus without other people noticing and it was a place she could stare at as we drove home, a way of steadying her breathing and keeping the tears at bay.

She smiled when she saw me. "What are you still doing here?"

"Waiting for you. Here." I handed her the flowers.

She took them. "Aw thanks Chris," she admired them for a moment and then looked up quizzically, "you aren't asking me out are you?"

I glared at her. "No."

She grinned. "It's just, I know how you are in love with me and all."

I rolled my eyes. "You know not everyone is in love with you Drue Potter."

The comment sobered her, "I know. Trust me."

I kicked myself, way to cheer her up. "No Drue, I didn't mean…"

"I know Chris. It's okay. Thanks for the flowers." Then Drue laughed. "But you know, flowers at my car, everyone is going to think you asked me out," she teased.

"You think we could fool them?" I asked continuing the game.

"Oooh, yes lets. Bet they wouldn't believe it though."

"Yeah because you would start laughing as soon as we told anyone."

"Would not!"

I just looked at her, "Drue."

She smiled guiltily. "Okay, you're right. It's just too weird. I would totally crack."

I sighed overdramatically. "Even after I brought you flowers."

"They are beautiful flowers," she conceded.

"Thanks. Although I totally didn't pick them out myself. They were pre-arranged."

"Well the pre-arranger did a lovely job."

"I'll be sure to let them know next time I go?"

She laughed. "Yes, definitely."

"Well I should go."

"Yeah me too. Dinner awaits."

"Always a pleasure."

Drue just rolled her eyes. I began to walk away. "Hey Chris," I turned. "Thanks."

I smiled "You're welcome."

I watched as Drue turned to her car and opened her bag for her keys. It was a search that began with vainly reaching in the front pouch of her bag and ended with Drue sitting on the pavement in front of her car, the entirety of her bag dumped out before her. I smiled to myself as I turned to my own car, there were some things that Drue would just never learn.

Drue started running. Long runs that took her away from her house. Away from her room where so many memories lingered, where so many tears had been shed, away from her parents, who lit candles and talked, who would hold hands one day only to not speak the next, away from her sister's emails and phone calls checking in, asking how Drue was doing and then going on to tell how perfect her life was all in the same breath.

Drue would run her feet pounding on the pavement, tears falling from her eyes, until she couldn't run any farther. Until her chest felt heavy and her legs ached. At those moments Drue found pure bliss, a euphoric only slightly less than when she cut. She could not cry for she did not have the breath, she could not think for she did not have the energy. All she could do was feel the pain in her chest as if no amount of air would ever be enough to fill it and the pain in her legs insuring her she had done well. It was pure bliss.

Drue sat in the back seat of the car tears streaming down her cheeks. She was tired, stressed, and overwhelmed. So despite hating herself for it, she cried. Once she started she couldn't stop. The tears felt to be never ending.

Her father turned around and saw her. "We are almost there. You can't go into the house crying."

Drue nodded silently.

When they arrived at their friend's house where they were to have dinner, her mother and father got out.

"Take five minutes and dry your face. Then I expect to see you inside," her father said. Then he slammed the door.

Drue watched her parents walk into the house. She tried to stop. She tried to think happy thoughts, she tried to steady her breathing, but nothing would stop the incessant tears from coming. "Stupid tears, stupid crying, I have to learn to be stronger," she said to herself as she reached into her purse and removed her razor. She pulled up the leg of her pants and made a cut. A single line across her knee, deep and clean. She focused her mind on the pain. And as she cleaned the blood, normal breathing returned.

In five minutes her face was cleaned and she was walking into the house to join her parents the only sign of her previous fall the slight glistening in the corner of her eyes.

She sat in her room with her textbook on her lap. It had been open to the same page for the last half hour. Every time she attempted to read she would make it a paragraph before her mind slid away from the text. She wasn't sure what she was thinking about just that she would look up to realize a half hour had gone by and she was still on the same page.

Drue knew how important this year was. She knew she had to work hard to keep her grades up. And most of the time, she liked the distraction. The forced attention on school work and projects. It gave her an excuse to get together with people or to sit in her room alone depending on her mood. But today she just couldn't focus. Her mind was flitting around from thought to thought, image to image, never stopping for long on any until at last it always came to rest on the same one - Roger. Roger sitting in the quad at lunch, a place she didn't even dare enter for the social fuxpex it would be making in the delicate balance with which the school functioned. And yet there he was, having moved up in the world from a band dork, to a drummer, to now a quad squader. He sat there with his new girlfriend surrounded by people, laughing, dancing, joking, and she had realized she no longer even recognized him. He was no longer the boy she had fallen for two years ago, or even the boy whom she had loved the year before. He had turned popular and in doing so he had gotten an ego. He now looked down upon people whom he never used to, he made fun of people in a way that verged on cruel instead of funny, and Drue had a sneaking suspicion that now when he strutted about it was for the eyes that turned his way rather than the laughs which had once been his goal. She missed her best friend, but no longer saw that person in the guy whom she watched every day at school. Sometimes, that made her miss him even more.

The phone rang jarring Drue instantly from her thoughts and causing her to silently curse herself when she realized that yet another twenty minutes had slipped by. She picked up the phone, "hello?"

"Drue?"

It was Stacey. Drue could recognize the tears brimming on her voice, and she braced herself for whatever drama her sister was about to communicate to her. "Stacey? What's wrong? You okay?"

"Yeah," her sister replied, breathing out deeply, "its just, well Andrew broke up with me and I don't know what to do. Drue what do I do?"

Drue almost laughed. Do? What did Stacey mean, do? You cried, you wallowed, what else was there? Into the phone Drue only sighed. "Oh Stacey, I'm so sorry! How'd it happen?"

"He just, well he was looking for the one, and I'm not ready for that. And I just…" Her sister continued to sob, "Drue, you've been through this, how do I get over him?"

Drue thought about it, what did she know about fixing broken hearts? What had she done? Cut. But that was hardly a desirable option. Run away; a little more appealing but not very practical. Keep on loving; the most realistic, but also the most painful. At last Drue just shook her head, "I don't know Stace, I just don't know."

"Well I should go." Her sister was breathing steadier now. "We have a meeting. I just needed to hear your voice. I just need to know it will be okay."

"It will," Drue answered hoping it was the truth. "Of course it will. It just takes time. It's going to be fine. I love you."

"I love you too," her sister responded and hung up.

Drue continued to hold the phone. It went dead and then the

dial tone sounded. Still Drue held the phone. She wondered if her sister really felt what she felt, if her sister really understood. On the one hand she hoped she did, she hoped that at last someone would understand what she was going through, how impossible it was to keep on living, how getting up every day was a fight in itself, and how every night she no longer had any dreams to wish for. She could hardly remember what life was like before this. What it meant to leave school and not instantly burst into tears, before she was so numb that there was hardly even room for self hatred, the only emotion she did feel at times. Mostly though, it was as if the world was going on around her and she was falling through it, falling and falling, desperately throwing her arms out for hand holds but just when she thought she saw one it would disappear, just a mirage, and so she would continue to fall as the world continued on without her. She wondered if now that her sister was falling too they might at least fall together. Yet, on the other hand she would never wish for her sister to end up down this rabbit's hole. She hoped that her sister would never have to know what this felt like. And so she held the phone unsure of what to do or what she should she wish for.

23

May 4th

Dear Espera,

I realized yesterday that I'm scared to be happy. Like I'm scared to let myself believe that life will actually ever treat me well again. Maybe that's good, maybe it leads to less disappointments, but it also restricts me from ever being completely happy. Because whenever I do get happy my brain has to come in and remind me I have no real reason for that happiness, that it won't last. I'm scared that I'll have to go through the last ten months again and if I lose anything right now I'll probably be back there. So I can't lose anything, which means I can't assume I have anything. I guess that's how I've changed. I used to assume everything would be ok and now everything is less sure. I can't afford to believe a fantasy. My happiness does not come as easily. But then, before I had Roger, so everything IS different anyway.

Love, Drue Potter

Drue had made it two months without cutting. She had never made it that long before. She was proud of herself. She wanted to have a party or at least celebrate but there was no one to invite, because no one knew. Instead, her parents held a family meeting. Drue hated family meetings. Her sister came home for a long weekend and so the whole family gathered in the living room to sit around a candle and talk. The idea was that the candle would make it easier, that somehow it would help them say things that couldn't be said around the dinner table or in the living room as they sat and chatted on a normal night.

Drue didn't quite see the logic in this but it seemed to work for the rest of the family. Her mom started and talked for fifteen minutes about what had been going on with her, then her dad started on his insights for twenty minutes, and then her sister talked for forty five minutes about the troubles in her head, and then all eyes fell on Drue. Drue stared back, saying nothing.

"Drue do you have something you'd like to add?" Her father asked gently.

"Nope," Drue said shaking her head.

"Well how do you feel about all this?" Her mom asked.

"I hate family meetings," Drue responded dumbly, it was all she could think of to say. She wanted to tell them that it was her two month celebration; she wanted them to congratulate her and tell her they were proud of her. But this meeting wasn't about her. It was about her parents. After eight months, they had decided it was time to enlighten their children. The thing was, Drue didn't care. Not really. Not anymore. She didn't want to have to fix her parents and so she didn't want to know they were broken. She didn't want to be included in an "adult conversation." She just wanted to be the daughter. She didn't want to have to comfort them when they cried, and she didn't want to know the reason for their tears. She wanted to be taken care of, not the other way around. I guess we have all just become selfish, she realized silently. Well, she was battling her struggles on her own, if she could take care of herself, surely her parents could do the same. We are all on our own now, she thought to herself.

Then she realized her family was still staring at her expectantly. "I hate family meetings," she repeated, "that is all I have to say."

Drue was humming to herself softly as she came in the door. It had been a good day; one of those rare occasions where she didn't leave school crying. Her father was waiting by the door. "We need to talk."

Drue looked at him questioningly. "Ok, just give me a second to put my bag down."

Her father followed Drue into her bedroom. Drue felt her heart pick up tempo, what could he need to tell her? What could have happened to make her father look so sombre?

"We found your story."

Drue froze, her bag half way to the floor. She slowly let it fall, unsure of what to do. The air in the room had become suddenly heavy and she felt her heart beat harder trying to make use of the limited oxygen. She had forgotten about her English assignment, she must have gotten careless, she must have left it out where her parents could read it, else.....

"Drue sit down," her father's voice brought her back.

Drue sat. "Daddy I'm sorry." A tear rolled down her cheek, "please don't be mad."

"We aren't mad Drue, just concerned. Do you think this is how we wanted to find out?"

It didn't take long for Drue to begin crying, "I never meant to disappoint you. I never wanted to cause you pain, I'm sorry."

Her father let Drue cry. He didn't put his arm around her and tell her it was going to be okay, he didn't tell her he loved her, or offer words of support; he just sat and watched her cry. So she cried. She cried and apologized and begged him not to tell Stacey. He didn't condemn her, or yell at her, but he never once asked her why, and that was punishment enough. He didn't care to know if she was better, despite the story ending happily, he didn't ask why she did it or say he was sorry if he had any part in the reasons. Instead, he just talked to her and then sat listening as she apologized for everything she could think of: for not being the perfect daughter, for reflecting badly on them, for failing them, for not being strong enough to hold it together like they expected her to. He never once said he forgave her, he never pretend to understand, or wonder how he never noticed his daughter was falling apart. He just let her cry. Finally there were no more tears. That's when he got up and extended a hand. "Come on, I'll take you driving. It will take your mind off things." He gave her a hug then.

They went driving. And it worked. For that hour all of Drue's thoughts consisted of finding the perfect moment to let up the clutch and what gear she was meant to be in. The wind felt good in her hair and her dad was patient. At the end of the lesson as they drove into the driveway Drue saw her mom's car. Drue could still see the look on her mother's face months before when she told Drue it would kill her to know Drue cut.

Next to her Drue's father felt her stiffen. "It's going to be okay," he said.

Drue's mother was waiting for them at the door. "Are you okay?" She asked.

Drue nodded. Her mother gave her a hug. That was it. No more was said. Drue was allowed to retire to her room.

That night she couldn't look at her parents the pain hurt so badly. The hurt in their eyes was so great she thought she'd explode. So she left. She didn't come to me that night. I wish she had, but it was still too soon. Instead, she sat in the parking lot of Kinko's and cried. Cried because she didn't know what else to do; her life had crumbled around her and she didn't know how to rebuild it.

Instead of me, she thought of the one person who she always went to when she was in tears. It didn't matter that they hadn't talked in months, she called, he said yes, and she went over. He let her sit on his bed and cry. He wanted her to promise she'd never do it again, she just wanted to forget. He told jokes, performed tricks and paraded around the room. It was like old times, before he got an ego, before he grew up. He played the part of the little kid who just wants everyone in the world to be happy. And it worked, at least a little, she smiled. She laughed.

"You know this means if I ever show up at your house terribly depressed I expect you to make a complete fool of yourself to cheer me up," he told her.

She smiled. "I am not as good as you at it, but I will most certainly try," she responded. She knew he never would. He would never tell anyone when he was hurt. He put everything in a box, and she knew, that especially now, especially with them hardly talking, he would never come to her. But the idea of it made her smile. She wished he needed her, just once. Just to know what that feeling was like.

When she returned home her parents looked at her. "Where were you?"

She hesitated, knowing the reaction his name would produce but she said it anyway, "Roger's".

Her mom stood up. "Sweetie do you really think that's a good idea? I mean he's what started all this in the first place."

Drue stared at her mother dumbfounded. Roger? Roger had started all this? She had to be kidding? Roger had been the one to save her that night, to give her at least that small amount of laughter, remind her the world had not ended. How dare her mother take from Drue the one thought that calmed her and steadied her, and brought breath back, the one thing that made this terrible night bearable. How could her mother be so cruel? Drue stared at her mother and said nothing, then she turned and returned to her room. She did not leave it again for the rest of the night.

She was told she'd get counselling, but the waiting list never turned into anything. She was sent to EMDR but when she stopped going she wasn't asked about it. In fact after that one day Drue's parents never brought up the subject again. Maybe they forgot. Or maybe they just choose to forget. Either way it left Drue on her own, again.

24

June 17th

Espera,

Why does it hurt so much? There is no validation. Every part of me, every bit from head to toe knows this is wrong. It's time to let him go and yet… and yet hope remains. As if, even after this long, I think he might just wake up tomorrow and realize he still loves me, that all the girls he's dated this year have not really meant anything. How can I possibly believe such things? Why do I still think of him? Stupid hope, gets me every time.

Love you, Drue.

It was supposed to be over. All of it, time was supposed to dissolve the pain. Then she glanced at her cuts, scars in various stages of healing that were scattered about her legs, arms, shoulders, and wrists. To hell with time. Time didn't solve anything, time just left her alone after everyone else had moved on. It wasn't her fault she thought angrily, it wasn't her fault anymore.

The glass hit the wall, hard. As hoped it shattered into thousands of pieces. She stared at the pieces for a long time. How beautiful the pieces looked, glistening there in the light. They almost looked innocent. Like me, she thought, almost innocent. She picked up a piece of glass, her piece: small, pretty and doing its best to reflect the image it was presented with. She turned the piece around looking at it from every angel. She pulled up her pant leg and stared at her leg looking for a clean place to cut. No, not her leg today, this piece of glass deserved better than that. She turned over her arm and stared at the clean skin just above her wrist. She made a quick cut, clean, simple. Not deadly, but deep. She sucked in her breath hard as the pain rushed through her. She made another cut next to the first. The world tilted dangerously from the pain. She let her breath out slowly. It stung, it numbed her thoughts. She sank to the floor, her back against the cupboards, the tile cold against her pant legs. She let the world swim about her. One more would do her in. She knew that. All she needed was to do the same thing to the other arm, a little harder, make sure to hit the vein and she would be done. She would have peace at last. She wondered idly if this was her destiny after all. If for all her talk of destiny and fate hers was to die here, in this room. If it wasn't, she reasoned, then I guess I was not as strong as God thought me to be. Another person I have failed. She almost smiled. It was almost funny really, how after leading such a perfect life she could end up so messed up. A shame. I'm sorry; she whispered softly, I'm sorry I couldn't be better, stronger. She played with the glass in her hand, wondering which decision took more strength, to make the final cut, or not to. She stared at her left arm, where the blood was dripping from her arm and onto the tile below. She watched the pool forming below her arm and she began to cry. She cried for him, she cried for herself, she cried for her weakness and failures and she cried for God. The God whom she wanted so much to believe in, but didn't understand, because He never seemed to be there when she needed Him the most. And then she cried for all those people who would miss her if she left. The crying didn't last long.

She got herself up, she washed her hands, she washed the floor, and cleaned up the glass. Her arm was now pink and stinging. She went and put on a long sleeve shirt wondering idly how long she would have to wear sweaters for.

Then she went into her room as if nothing at all had happened. After all, her parents would be home soon.

Drue's sister came home for the summer. Drue was excited; she was excited about the prospect of having her best friend back in her life, of returning to life as it used to be. She hoped maybe she could just go back to being her sister's shadow again. But then her sister came home. And it was nothing like it had been.

Stacey did not need Drue the way she used to and Drue, in turn, had not realized how she had gotten used to living independently, how she came and went without telling people where she was going or with whom. While her parents continued not to notice these things, her sister did. She'd ask Drue. Drue didn't always want to answer.

Additionally, Stacey had lost weight. Like 50lbs of weight and for a girl who was never overweight to begin with, it made her appear small and sickly. It also made Drue feel fat. Not just her normal, "I'd like to lose some weight", but actually fat. Drue and her sister had been the same weight their entire lives and now Drue felt she would break Stacey just by hugging her. Drue towered over her big sister, dominating any picture they were in together, and she could no longer borrow her clothes. Drue knew something was wrong. She knew no one would want to look that small, and she knew her sister wasn't anorexic. But it didn't matter. Her entire life Drue had striven to be like her sister and even if she knew she shouldn't want to look like that, she did. In Drue's head, that's all there was too it. The fact that she didn't, meant that she was doing something wrong.

Drue went on a diet. When that didn't make a dent in the fifty pound difference Drue tried to eat less. She would wake up every day look in the mirror and tell herself she was fat. She would make herself hate how she looked so that she would have the strength to get through the day without caving in and eating too much. Soon these morning sessions didn't take long, the self-hatred became part of Drue's daily life. Just another thing to add to her list. She was weak and fat.

Drue could hardly remember a time when anything else was true.

SENIOR YEAR: The End

"Life isn't about finding yourself. It is about creating yourself."

- unknown

PRESENT DAY: NOVEMBER

" I dunno, the whole year is just kind of a blur. I wish I could offer you more than that. I wasn't even really writing much."

"I know I looked at the journals, you have months where you wrote nothing."

"That's the point! It was as if I was on this intense medication that made all of life just a little bit blurry. All I remember is what it felt like to wake up every morning and hate myself. What it felt like to cut every few weeks because the loneliness was so complete. But actual events? God, I don't know."

I stare at Drue speechless. She sits looking out the window. The sounds of the coffee shop descend upon us, the clinking of glasses, the conversation amongst friends, the calling out of orders. Drue continues staring out the window, unaware of the people around us, or even, so it seems, of me. At last she looks at me and begins again.

"I was trying to find myself, but I didn't know that was what I was doing. I quit band because I knew it was bad for me, but I didn't know that I had to walk away from that organization in order to see who I was without it. I got new friends, I did new things, I kept myself busy. But I still remember sitting at the park and crying most afternoons. I didn't understand how God gave him so much joy and gave me so little. I didn't understand how I could still not be better yet. That's all I remember about senior year. I was waiting for my miracle, preparing myself to be happy again, the only thing is, it never came. I was happy for moments, I laughed more, I had more fun, but that miracle that I was hoping for? It never came." Then she laughs bitterly, "Once you are given all your dreams, you think that's the norm. You think that perfect comes more than once in lifetime." She smiles sadly at me, "it takes a long time to be satisfied with just pockets of perfection, to find happiness in the simpler things of life once more. That's what I was doing senior year. Not much of a story there, huh?"

I touch her hand lightly, but she pulls it away. I don't press.

25

September 2nd

Dear __

I shall name you Scarlette. After Scarlette O'Hara. I think I'd like to be Scarlette O'Hara. I mean as much as you spend so much time hating her and as much as she hurt others and gets hurt at least she's always true to herself. She's bold and brash and does what she wants without a second thought to those around her.

But then, maybe not. Maybe it had nothing to do with her, maybe she, like everyone else, was just doing what she had to, in order to get through another day. In the end, even she got broken. Is no one safe, then? Is there any way to not get hurt? How do I learn to guard my heart that much? And then, if I do, would I still be me?

Love, Drue Potter

Drue dropped out of band. She knew that she would not be able to make it another year of seeing him every day, seeing the new freshman girls fawn over him. She didn't cry for him anymore, she could watch him with other girls and not feel like she was being punched in the stomach. Still, that didn't make her strong enough to get through another band season with him. So as much as I begged and pleaded with her to stay, she just left. She left the place which had been her home for the past three years, left the family that she had created for herself. She walked away without looking back. She spent her second periods at a coffee shop now, doing homework or reading, and trying not to think about what she was leaving behind.

It was here that she met Brad.

She was reading for history. She sat in the tall back arm chair that was her favourite at the coffee shop. It was off in one corner, surrounded by bookshelves on two sides, so that, other than the small table and other chair that sat beside her own, she was virtually secluded. Usually, people would see she was doing her work and leave her alone, which allowed her to block out the sounds of their talking, the clicking of glasses, the clang of the espresso machine, or the beeps as cars were locked outside. In her corner Drue could block out the rest of the world and bury herself in her book as she was doing today. She could never quite recall what aspect of European History she was reading about that day, but she remembers enjoying it. She was unusually absorbed, so much so that she hardly noticed the tall dark young man who entered her corner.

"May I sit here?" He asked gently.

Drue looked up distracted. It took a moment for her to focus on the boy in front of her, and when she did she mostly noticed his bright red hat which stood out against his dark skin. "Sure," she said absently and returned to her reading.

The boy sat down on the chair opposite hers and took out his own book. "What are you studying for?" He asked her.

Drue looked up. "History," she replied simply.

"Do you go to school around here?" He asked then.

Drue let out a sigh a bit annoyed at the distraction. "Yeah, at the High School," she said nodding in the direction of campus, "you?"

"City College," he replied.

She nodded in approval and then returned to her reading. They worked in silence. Drue looked up once and found the boy watching her. She frowned slightly and returned to her book. When she looked up again a few minutes later, he seemed to be deeply engrossed in his book, so she went back to her reading, unperturbed.

At noon, Drue began to put her books away.

"Time to go back?" He asked.

She nodded. "Yep, breaks over."

She picked up her backpack. "Well, it was nice meeting you," she said turning to go.

"Yeah you too," he held out his hand, "Brad," he added.

"Drue."

He paused, then added, "hey so I'm having a party on Friday. You should come. Bring a friend if you'd like. It will be fun." He hurriedly wrote something on a scrap of paper and handed it to Drue. "Here's my number and the address, call me or just stop by."

Drue took the paper, looked at it dumbly for a moment then stuffed it in her pocket and left.

"Well what do you think?" Drue asked looking at me expectantly. She sat on my bed the English homework she had been working on still spread out before her.

"What do I think? I think you'd be crazy to go," I responded, "I mean why would you want to go to a college party? You don't drink."

Drue shrugged, "I know, it's just. Well I could use some new friends. And maybe it'd be fun. I mean, aren't you curious? Just a little."

I shook my head. "No," I responded.

"Oh." Drue looked down. "Well I am."

I looked at her. She stared at her hands, "I'll go with you, if you really want," I finally said.

She looked at me, her eyes lit up. "Really? 'Cause that'd be really cool. And we don't have to stay that long, honest. I just want to see it. That's all."

"Yeah, okay," I agreed warily.

She parked the car and we stared in front of us. "Maybe this is a bad idea."

I looked at her. "Well we are here now."

"I know it's just," she paused, "maybe we shouldn't."

"Yeah, maybe not."

She glared at me. "A lot of help you are. Come on let's go."

She got out of the car. I followed. The house was in a small cul-de-sac. It was a cute two story stucco house that didn't instantly scream college frat house until one noticed the open garage door which held a keg and a group of scruffy looking guys circled around it. One of them smiled as we approached, "hey hey."

Drue smiled back. "Hey."

They offered her a beer, she shook her head, they turned to me, I also shook my head. "Driving," I lied. They nodded.

Drue wandered into the house. She walked through it, and then quickly came back out. "Okay, I came, I saw, let's go."

I smiled. "Fine by me."

We started to leave. Just as we reached the end of the driveway someone called Drue's name. She turned. I felt, more than saw her smile. "Hey."

A boy came up and gave her a hug. She turned to me. "This is Brad. Brad, Chris."

He held out his hand to me. He put a beer in Drue's hand.

"Come on, you can't be leaving yet."

She looked at me with a small shrug. She allowed herself to be steered back into the house. I followed reluctantly.

The downstairs looked just as we had left it a few minutes before. A group of guys by the fridge rummaging for the perfect beer, some girls dancing in the corner by the stereo and in front of the TV sat an odd disarray of people who looked completely lost as to where they were at all. Brad however, ignored all this and instead led Drue upstairs grabbing a beer as he passed the kitchen with the hand that he wasn't around Drue shoulders.

Brad's room was nice enough. It was clean at least, and the music wasn't quite so pounding. Drue plopped down on Brad's bed and I sat down next to her. Brad opened the beer he had grabbed from the kitchen and joined us. Drue contemplated the beer Brad had handed her earlier, she turned the cup in her hand, looking at it, smelling it and then at last with a shrug more to herself than anyone else, she took a sip. She made a face, but quickly wiped the look off her face and took another sip.

It was then that I knew it was going to be a long night.

While Brad talked, Drew drank her beer. Then, she drank another one. And another. Around Drue's fourth beer a friend of Brad's came up into the room. He didn't say anything and yet Brad went and began rummaging about in his drawer, soon he was set up. He looked at us, "You want some?"

Drue's eyes went wide. She shook her head, and leaned over to me. "Is that coke?" She asked quietly.

I shrugged and whispered back, "how should I know?" Then I added, "are you ready to go yet? This is getting uncomfortable."

She laughed. "But the world is so beautiful!"

I rolled my eyes. "Only because you are drunk. Come on, please?"

She scowled at me. "Fine let's go. I just need to say goodbye." Drue pushed herself up. She swayed. "Oh shit." She said softly.

I took her shoulders. "Come on Drue."

She nodded. "Yes, right. Let's go." We were almost out the door when she remembered. "But I haven't said goodbye!" She turned around. Brad was bent over the table with his friend. She walked over and placed a hand on his back, "I just wanted to say bye." He turned around.

"You're leaving?"

She nodded.

"Why? It's still early."

She let out a small breath. "My friend wants to get home."

"Oh alright, can I see you again?"

She shrugged. "Yeah okay," she gave him her number.

When he had put it in his phone he gave her a hug. "Ok then. Have a good night. Be safe."

She laughed. "Will do. See ya around." She gave a wave and then came back to where I was waiting at the door. "Ok, now we may go."

"Alright." I led her down the steps and helped her into the car. I drove us to the wharf.

"The beach!" Drue ran throwing herself onto the sand as if meeting a long lost friend. I came up and sat down beside her. "God I love the beach," she said falling onto her back and looking up at the sky. "Wish I knew the constellations better," she mused, quietly.

The waves crashed in front of us like thunder in the quiet night. We lay in silence listening to the waves, letting the sound wash over us as the water did the sand, sobering us up physically and mentally from the evening. At last she spoke again, "I had fun tonight."

"Why?" I asked sitting up and looking at her, "you didn't do anything fun."

She sat up too, brushing the sand from her hair as she did so. "I laughed," she said looking at me, "it's been a long time since I've laughed. I liked it."

I nodded. "Come on, let's get you home." I extended a hand, she let me pull her up and take her home.

That was enough. That was all it took. Drue found ways to get herself invited to parties. She found people to drag along, sometimes me, but not often. She began drinking every weekend; it was her way of escape. And during the week, she would cut. It was all just part of the routine of dealing.

Drue's mother had always told Drue if you pretend to be happy, you will be. So Drue tried. With all her might, she would pull herself out of bed every morning and plant a smile on her face. She'd go through her day at school, lonely and in a daze, smiling, hoping to make it through. Then on the weekends she would drink and it wouldn't be so hard to be happy. She let herself be swept up by the world of college parties. A world where for the first time in her life Drue was considered pretty, she had friends and when she walked into a room, boys wanted to talk to her. Drue enjoyed it. She'd tell me the stories of the parties she went to, the people she was meeting, and the boys she had kissed. As the year went on the lists grew.

But sometimes at night she would still cry for him. There were other boys now, new crushes, new kisses, but sometimes at night he would still appear. She would lie in bed and wonder if she would ever find another boy like that. If she would ever fall in love again. She wondered how he was, what he was doing. She wished she could call, but knew she could not.

She hoped he was happy.

26

September 10th

Scarlette,

I don't know if I can live without him. I mean, yeah, I'm breathing and going through the motions of life, but living? Surely that ended the day he left. That was the day I stopped laughing, that I stopped knowing pure joy, that I stopped being special and loved in his eyes.

I wonder if someone else will be able to ever give that feeling to me again. If I will ever again be complete, full, and not with this awful emptiness inside...... Bed.

Drue.

Drue started a new job. It was catering and she was excited. She liked the idea of working fun events, of meeting new people. But on the first day as she showed up to the event location, she was nervous. She held her hands behind her back, squeezing them together tightly, as if all her nerves could be directed to that one spot. She looked for the woman she was supposed to report to. Instead she saw only a boy sitting at one of the tables folding napkins. She walked up to him. "Hi." The word came out hesitantly.

The boy turned, smiling. "Hi," he responded extending his hand, "I'm Bryan."

The boy had the widest eyes Drue had ever seen. They were a deep brown that overpowered the rest of his features. Drue saw only kindness in those eyes. She took his hand. "Drue."

"So you're new here, huh?"

Drue nodded. "Starting tonight."

"Well, welcome," Bryan said with a slight laugh, "here, you can help me do roll ups." He pushed some napkins and silverware towards her. "It's tons of fun." he said with a roll of his eyes.

Drue smiled. Maybe working here wouldn't be so scary after all.

"She's a bitch for sure."

"Not necessarily," he responded.

"No, for sure. All beautiful girls are bitches."

"True, but she may not realize she is a beauty."

"That's a thought. But how could she not realize she is beautiful? She'd have to be blind."

"Or very naive, but even still, it is possible. She isn't the conventional beauty."

"I dunno. I think she knows" his friend said unconvinced.

"Well, there is only one way to find out." He got up.

The boy that was walking toward Drue had short blond hair that fell about his face in disarray. However, the dishevelled look suited this boy who had the most brilliant blue eyes Drue had ever seen. As he approached where she sat on the couch talking to a girlfriend he smiled and she saw that he had a single dimple on his left side, giving him the appearance of being slightly younger than his twenty years, but which also made the boy seem charming despite his laid back air. She smiled back. He sat down and extended a hand. "I'm Quinn."

"Drue," she said taking his hand. "Nice to meet you."

She sat towards the back of the room. She lined her pencils up in a neat row in front of her. She took her calculator out and put it beside her. She also had a bottle of water and a pack of mints on her desk. "Mints are good", her mother had told her, "they help wake up your mind". So there they were the little blue and white tin of peppermints her mom had handed her in a hurry the morning before, an afterthought to her mother's own day, but still a comforting reminder that her parents did in fact know what day it was for Drue. She breathed in deeply, waiting.

She filled out the bubbles delicately; this was always Drue's favourite part. She wrote her name, her birthday, her race. Carefully, precisely, Drue took her time to make the bubbles look just perfect on her form. She liked how her name looked in bubbles, how the "P" and "R" were almost directly across from each other and then the design shot upward and then came to settle with the two "Ts" in the middle. Drue liked the precision, the balance of it. It calmed her to see her name written like that: balanced, perfect and undistinguishable from anyone else's in the family. She pretended the test was not hers, but Stacey's. She glanced at all the bubbles that sat blank. If this were Stacey's test, the majority of those would be filled in to the correct answer. Every answer in the verbal would be correct, every bubble filled in to the right space. She knew at the end of her exam it would not look nearly as nice, every answer would not be correct. But for now, right at this moment, she had scored 100%. She liked this moment.

Then the test began. Drue opened her booklet and started. She hoped the classes she had taken in preparation would pay off. She hoped she would do okay. But then she stopped hoping and got swept up in the exam. She liked the challenge; she liked pushing her brain and forcing herself to think about things in other ways. The time went by quickly.

It was only at the end of the test as Drue picked up her pencils, her calculator, her water, and her mints, that Drue began to get nervous. What if she had been wrong about that problem with the triangles? She had never been good at geometry, she had always just had Roger help her, she hadn't actually learned anything in that freshman class. And what about that analogy about the king and the hillside? Was she right to have skipped that analogy with the word she had never heard before? Thoughts raced through her mind, doubts pulsed through her body.

She reached her car and sat down resting her head against her steering wheel. She breathed in again and again, trying to tell herself there was nothing she could do now, it was over, done. And if she had done really badly, well, there was always next time.

Still, she hoped she had done well. It was, after all, her SATs.

A few weeks later Drue saw Quinn again. She was sitting on a couch next to a girl she barely knew and she was bored. She twirled her hair around her finger wondering how she would amuse herself for the night, when all of a sudden she saw him. She couldn't be sure that it was the same boy she had met a few weeks before, so she kept glancing over. She thought he was doing the same, because every once in awhile their eyes would meet, just for a moment before both glanced away quickly.

The girl beside Drue also noticed him. "Oh, he's cute," Drue heard the girl say.

Drue felt a shy smile crease her lips. He was cute, there was something about his smile, the way it lit up his face and gave him a boyish joy that was refreshing. His eyes danced and it was at that moment that she formed a crush on this boy. Just like that, a moment, a second.

"Be right back," the girl next to Drue said getting up. Drue watched her walk away, wondering if it was really that easy.

Drue looked around the room. It was still early, it would get better. She needed another beer. She got up.

When she returned to her seat the other girl was already there. "He has a girlfriend," she whined.

Drue raised her eyebrows. "Really? Did you ask him?" She asked calmly, silently cursing.

"No, but I asked a friend of his. Apparently some girl from Back East."

"Hmmm.... Shame," Drue asserted.

"Indeed," the other girl agreed.

Drue marked the new boy off her list, but that did not mean she couldn't become his friend.

"Hey."

"Hey," her response was as simple as my greeting. Then there was silence.

"Whatiya doing?"

"I'm attempting this math problem. Why the heck didn't you take AP Stats with me? You really could have been helpful right about now."

I laughed. "Yeah, cause you know how I've always been better at math than you."

I felt her smile on the other end of the phone "Yeah well, any help would be useful right about now. This totally sucks." I heard her close the book. "That's it. I'm done. I can't do it." There was shuffling as she got up and went from where she had probably been working, sprawled out on her bedroom floor, to her rocking chair where she often sat to talk on the phone. After a moment she began again, "so what's up with you?"

"Not much. How'd your SATs go?"

"Eh, okay I guess. They are done at least. What about you?"

"Eh, same."

She laughed. "Yep that pretty much sums *that* experience up."

I smiled, "so, how are you otherwise? How are your parents?"

"Same. They are beginning to notice me again, so that's an improvement."

"And your sister?"

"Still at college."

"Right. "

"I don't miss her as much anymore. I guess I'm getting use to it."

"And you? How are you?"

She knew what I was asking about. She never admitted that she was a self-mutilator, and I never said that she cut, we didn't put a name on what she did, somehow that would make it too real. Instead it was always kept vague, in the background, but it didn't keep me from checking up on her. And she didn't evade the question. "Actually really good."

"Really?"

"Yeah. I think I'm done. I cleaned out all my razors yesterday. I've decided I don't need them, so I've gotten rid of them all. It's been a month and ten days."

"Wow, very nice."

"Yeah, I thought so."

"Hey!" Drue's face broke into a smile as she saw Bryan walk into the door. "I didn't know you were working today."

"In the flesh," he said with a smile.

"How have you been? Been awhile."

"Yeah, I've been here. Where have you been?"

Drue made a face. "School."

"But it's your senior year, aren't you supposed to slack off senior year?"

"You would think right? But no, turns out you actually have to work hard still. Hey grab one of those, would you?" She nodded at one of the boxes lined up by the bar. Bryan picked one up and they walked outside.

"So have you started the whole application process yet?"

Drue rolled her eyes. "Just starting. Kinda slow going though."

"Yeah. I never was much a fan of that process myself. Luckily all the UC Schools had the same application. Makes the processes a little easier."

"Definitely a saving grace," Drue agreed.

"Where are you applying?"

Drue shrugged. "Anywhere that will get me out of here."

"So not Stanford, huh?"

Drue made a face: "Too hard."

Bryan raised his eyebrows.

"Bryan!" Drue and Bryan both turned. Their boss strolled towards them. "Glad you could make it. Would you mind going and setting up the second bar? It's going to be over on the patio there. All the alcohol should be in the back pantry."

Bryan nodded. "Yep absolutely." He gave a small nod to Drue. "See ya later."

"Of course." Drue turned in the opposite direction to finish setting up the buffet.

The first time it happened was three days later. She was standing in her room and all of a sudden she couldn't breathe. She sank to the floor trying to regain control, trying to fill her lungs, too stunned to even understand what was happening. She concentrated on her breathing, trying to get enough oxygen to her lungs such that her vision might return, that the world might right itself once more, but then the panic started.

Her stomach clenched, her mind became hazy and vision was almost entirely lost. Only one thought became clear, amongst all the fog, perfectly spelled out in her mind, she needed her razor. But then the panic deepened. She did not have a razor. She had gotten rid of them all. She had thought if she did not have them, she would not need them. But as she lay there on the floor she wondered what she was suppose to do now.

She slowly got up, her hands shook, she tried to steady them. She walked to her purse; surely she had not gotten rid of them all. She picked up the first bag. Her hands searched all the normal spots, the hidden crevices and pockets where Drue kept her razors so they couldn't be found. Each turn was empty. The world tilted around Drue as her vision blurred. She put out a hand to steady herself but nothing was there. She sank to the floor dragging another bag with her. She searched this bag, feeling, groping, for the familiar prick as her finger found the razor, but no prick came. The bag was empty. So was the next. And the next.

Drue's hands were numb and she watched herself as if not part of her body. She went through the motions, her alarm rising as each bag turned up empty.

When she finished the last bag, she returned to her body but felt only terror. Tears were now streaming down her face, her vision was blurred, and she glanced about her room frantically. Breathing came in short gulps. I am drowning, she thought mildly, drowning on air. She spotted her open desk drawer and moved to it hurriedly. She did not know what she hoped to find there, only that maybe; just maybe, it held some salvation.

A mere five feet away the distance felt like eternity as she scrambled to reach it. Drue did not notice the chair in front of her until she tripped over it, sending her to the floor, clothes flying and a sharp cracking sound as her head hit the corner of the desk. Drue didn't notice the pain; all of her attention was focused on her destination - her final hope.

She rummaged through her drawer no longer aware of her own motions. Each item was picked up, run across her wrist in vain hope and then thrown aside when it did nothing to focus her now spinning world. Pens, scissors, letter openers, more pens, pencils, paper clips, they all came out and were soon on the floor across the room. Then at last, she saw it. A beautiful finely pointed protractor! She removed the metal object and ran it hard across her arm. No blood appeared, she did it again, still no blood. But her racing heart slowed a beat and her breathing became recognizable. There was a puckered red line on her arm. No blood, but a dull ache pulsed through her.

Drue sank to the floor falling into her body and looked about herself as if seeing the room for the first time. The room was a mess: her single chair lay on its side and her small floor was a disarray of clothes, bags and pens. She buried her face in her hands and tried to catch her breath. Deep breaths in and out, in and out, until at last her hands stopped shaking and her vision returned.

Then she just sat in silence, for a long time. That day Drue went and got a new packet of razors. She had to go to three stores, and after each store she wondered if this meant God was telling her something. She wondered if she really needed them. But then she found them. When she returned to her room, now cleaned and returned to normal she hid the packet in her sock draw. She never wanted to be so helpless again.

27

September 30th

Dear Scarlette,

I've gained weight again. And I'm trying to be okay with this fact. That my body's changing and whatnot, but I can't. As a little girl you are programmed to look up to your big sister and mother. Especially me, especially the baby. So how do I become okay with being the only one in the family with curves? With a butt and breasts and hips? How do I convince myself that this is normal and beautiful when everything else is telling me otherwise? I like my shoulders, that's it. But it's a start, right?

I'm really awful at dieting. I seem to forget that what you eat, actually affects how much weight you gain. Like there is no cause and effect in my head. Hmmmmm, quite the problem.

I gotta get to work. Hope Bryan's working tonight.

Later. Drue

To get herself away from school, a place she had begun to dread more than any other, Drue signed herself up for City College classes. Thus it was that every Tuesday and Thursday Drue found herself walking to class, staring out at the ocean and wondering what it would be like to actually be in college, to have all of the High School drama behind her and to know that she was at last free from it all. She loved this place: the ocean, the palm trees, the sun that showed constantly and the gentle breeze that was always blowing in from the sea. Still, she didn't plan to miss it next year. She was going to get as far away from this place as she could. No California school would suffice; she was going to the East Coast. She was going to get out of this town.

It was this thought that was consuming Drue's mind that Thursday afternoon as she walked to her astronomy class. It was then that she saw Quinn. She looked like shit that day, but she hadn't planned on seeing him. She hadn't seen him in a few days, and then it had only been at parties. She had never seen him at school before! But just like that, he walked past.

Her mind was slow to recognize him, so was his. She said "hey" and he returned the greeting. Then both walked on without looking back. However, they might as well have talked for hours, the way her body reacted, her stomach clenched up and her throat became dry. She didn't understand this feeling. She wasn't supposed to like him this much, not this time. Not now. Not after all she had been through. She would give anything to have this boy like her. The idea hit her, hard. She knew this feeling too well, and she hated it. She liked herself, she liked who she had become, she didn't want to change for some boy, but she knew she would. And that idea scared her.

The phone rang. I looked at the clock. Two eleven, right on time. I picked it up.

"Hi!" Her voice was dancing on the other end of the line.

"Hi Drue." I responded sighing, I knew what this meant.

"How are you?"

"I'm good Drue, how are you?"

"I am sooo good!" She said laughing. "Whata up to?"

I couldn't help but smile. "It's two in the morning Drue, what do you think I am up to? I was on my way to bed."

"Oh." She was quiet for a moment.

"Do you need me to come get you?"

I could feel her grin through the phone. "Awww, Chris! Could you? Thank you so much. That would be so amazing!"

"Where are you?"

"Uh." Her voice went flat. "Well, hmmmm." There was a pause, "Allison, where are we?"

"Dame Street." I heard her friend tell Drue.

"Dame Street" Drue repeated into the phone. "Right next to the High School."

"Okay. I'll call you when I get there."

"Thannnnk you!" Drue sang and then hung up.

I let out an audible breath gathering up my coat and keys. These night time calls were becoming all too routine.

Drue was jumping about the street corner when I arrived. She grinned and waved wildly at me, climbing into the front seat. "Hello, Hello!"

"You know you really shouldn't make a point of standing on the street corner in this neighbourhood."

"Chris, do I really look like a prostitute to you?" I gave a quick glance over her short skirt, halter top and large hoop earrings, I raised my eyebrows. "Ok, don't answer that," she conceded. "The point is I would never sell myself for money."

"No, only for free drink," Allison piped up from the backseat.

"Would not!" Drue returned. "Maybe free entrance into a club." Drue grinned at me. "Just kidding."

"Did you have a good night?" I asked.

"Oh the very best. It was so much fun. Wasn't it?" Drue turned to Allison to validate this point which she did with an enthusiastic nod.

"Definitely, Drue met a new boy!"

I raised an eyebrow. "Not a new boy," Drue corrected, "Quinn. I've met him loads before. Just haven't gotten him to kiss me yet. But don't worry, I'll get there." She grinned.

"Yeah and meanwhile she'll just make out with every other guy at the party."

"Did not!"

Allison rolled her eyes.

"You live right along here, right?" I asked Allison.

"Yeah, this next one with the gate out front. Thank you so much Chris. This really was amazing of you."

"Yeah, no problem."

Allison climbed out of the car.

I turned to Drue, "home?"

Drue made a face. "Do we have to?"

"Yeah, kind of. We have school tomorrow. Or today rather. You have to be up in four hours Drue, I think it'd be best I get you home."

"Oh." Drue laid her head back on the chair. "School is going to suck tomorrow, isn't it?"

"For you? Probably."

"Damn."

"Drue?" She rolled her head to look at me. "Are you happy? Like does this make you happy?"

She shrugged. "I don't know. I guess. Maybe." Then quietly, so quietly that I almost missed it, she said, "I miss Roger."

I looked at her. I saw a small tear on her cheek. I didn't say anything else until we reached her house. She climbed out. "Thanks Chris. I'm really sorry to always bother you like this."

"It's okay. I'm here," I answered.

I watched her stumble to her door, watched her scramble for her keys, made sure she got into the house okay. Then I left.

She walked into work and instantly spotted Bryan. His back was to her and he was talking to the cooks, but Drue knew it was him. She had come to know the tilt of his head when he talked and the way he rolled the collar of his work shirt. Drue smiled pleased he was working tonight. He had not been there last week and the party had not been the same without his easy laughter and sarcastic comments, his gentle teasing, not to mention his expertise knowledge.

Drue walked over to him. "Hey."

He turned. "Hey yourself. How are you?"

Drue shrugged. "Fine, we missed you last week." Drue took some silverware and began rolling.

He came over to join her. "Yeah, I went away for the weekend…"

She would keep thinking she was done with it. She would keep thinking she had quit. Sometimes she would write in her journal she had quit, another time she told her friends, but the cutting had become an addiction and so it always drew her back. She would be fine, then all of a sudden the sun would grow dimmer, the air thicker and she would have trouble breathing. Her stomach would ache and tears would threaten at all hours of the day. It was then that the world of cutting would engulf her once more. Sometimes it was a boy, sometimes getting on the scale, other times all it took was to have no one to sit with at lunch. Then the razor would come out of its draw and she would cut. Not often, but enough. She continued her habit.

It was in one of these bad spells, as Drue came to think of them, that she finally got help. She was saying her prayers after cutting for the first time in a month and half. An **x** that crossed her wrist in a distortion of perfection. Her parents had scolded her that day for not being on top of her applications and she had failed another Spanish test. It wasn't much, but it was enough. She had been tired, and overworked, and still had a stack of homework to do. She knew she needed to focus, and couldn't. So she cut.

Now she lay saying her prayers, fingering the scar lightly when it came to her in a strength unparallel with anytime before that. Not that she needed help, or that this was wrong, but that she couldn't do it alone. That she had to go and ask for someone to be on her side. And this was the grace of God; this phantom hand that helped her out of bed and led her down the street to where a friend lived. Drue had only known this girl for a few weeks, but there was something in this girl's eyes that promised understanding and so Drue found herself walking the short block and a half to her house on that dark November night. She was almost there when she decided this was stupid, that you don't go over randomly to someone's house at ten at night. She started to turn back, but then she felt a tug, a pull, and a knowledge that she had to do this, now, before she lost the courage. She understood that for some reason this was very important. And so she made herself continue on, telling herself that if all the lights were out in the house, she wouldn't have to knock. But the lights were on and when Drue knocked, her friend answered the door.

"Hey!" She said brightly.

"Hey." Drue's voice was soft, wavering just slightly.

"What's wrong, you ok?"

Drue breathed in deeply. The fog she had been in began to fade, the presence of God softened. She became more of herself. That scared her.

"I have a big favour to ask," she began unsteadily. She had thought about what to say, but it sounded inadequate now. In the full year and three months since this had all began, she had never asked help of anyone, much less someone she barely knew. She didn't exactly go around telling people she cut. This was hers to deal with.

"Trouble at home? You want to sleep here?" Her friend smiled. It was an offer that she had often posed to Drue and Drue had often taken. But it was not what she had come for tonight.

Drue gave a weak imitation of the girl's smile. "No, it's bigger than that."

"What?"

Drue bit her lip. "Will you come to counselling with me? Or like take me? Because see my parents sent me once but after like two sessions I just stopped going and they dropped it," she said it all in one breath, as if a single pause would mean she wouldn't make it through.

"Yeah of course. Is it something specific? Or just like in general?

Drue stood silent for a moment. "If I tell you, will you promised not to tell any one or to change your opinion of me?"

The girl smiled. "Of course not."

Drue pulled back her sleeve. The scar was already healing. It wasn't so gruesome looking now, just a small cut really, innocent … almost. She looked up at her friend, hoping for kindness and yet needing scolding.

The girl looked only briefly. "Ok, so why do you do it? Are there reasons or just like general shit?"

"There are so many reasons. School, parents, boy stuff, I dunno." Drue moved uncomfortably, this wasn't easy anymore. Where was God now?

The girl looked at Drue again. "Can I ask you one thing? Is it clean? Like do you do it with something clean?"

Drue smiled. She remembered her first time. "Yeah, they're clean. Bought for that purpose."

The girl met Drue's eyes. "You'll be fine. You're a good girl. And I'll make sure you go. Do you want me to call or just come along…..?"

"Just make sure I go through with it, that I don't chicken out."

"Alright, it will all be fine ya know. Have a good night sweetie." She gave Drue a hug and kiss and watched as Drue walked away. Drue's smile faded as she did.

Drue got back to her room and drew in a breath. Well this didn't feel so good after all. Now her secret was exposed. Now she was found out. She needed to be punished. As much as she knew it was wrong, she had to do it anyway. If she was going to stop she'd best get one more time in. Besides what she had done was wrong. She shouldn't burden others. She took a razor from her bedside table, looked at it only for a moment before making two cuts deep into her arm. They stood next to each other, two parallel lines deep with blood. They bled onto her pyjamas but she was too tired to move. So she lay in her bed and felt the blood leaving her. She did not need to look at the cuts to know these were the deepest she had ever made. But then, that had been the point. For these were to be her last cuts and when they healed she was meant to be done, and she still needed some time. She would just have to take it one step at a time. Starting, she thought to herself, with sleep.

She rolled over and closed her eyes.

29

October 11th

Dear Scarlette,

My dream from last night:

I was visiting Stacey at school. We were in the parking lot outside of the sorority trying to head out to dinner. I came upon the car and Stacey was already in the passenger seat. I remember being a little annoyed, it was true that it was more my car, but Stacey could have at least offered. Reluctantly I climbed into the car and turned on the ignition. As I put the car in drive and stepped on the gas, the car began backing up. I stared at the controls; sure enough the car had been put in reverse, not drive. I cursed myself for being so stupid, and then switched it back to drive and began again. However, I still backed up, and this time it was fast. We flew by cars on our left and right. Luckily no one had parked directly behind us. I remember looking behind me and seeing nothing. I felt only panic as once again we sped by a line of cars in reverse. At least we were heading toward the exit, I thought, however unconventionally, we were getting there. Still, it'd be much easier in drive, or at least if I could just see where I was going. Instead we continued backward blindly in short bursts of speed. Stopping and starting and jumping more than driving.

"Drue, what are you doing?" Stacey finally demanded.

"I don't know!" I cried back my voice cracking. I tried again, and again we shot backwards.

Just then a cop pulled into the parking lot. I wasn't sure if jumping backwards was illegal but I wasn't about to find out. "You drive." I said at last giving up. I put the car in park and got out.

Stacey climbed over the seat, put the car in drive and calmly, easily, turned the wheel and steered out of the parking lot. I could only watch in exasperated silence.

Then I woke up. Dunno what it means, your guess would be as good as mine. That's all for now.

Drue.

He saw her across the green. She was sitting on a bench writing in her journal. He walked over. She glanced up as he approached, smiled.

He liked her smile. It lit up her face, it contained innocence and sweetness. It reminded him of the kindness still in the world. He forgot sometimes. His life had not been easy; there had been hardships, sadness, and struggles. Things, he thought looking at the curly haired girl in front of him, that she had never experienced. He liked that, her naivety of life's pains. Well that, and she was hot. He laughed at himself as he thought it, but it was true. No guy would disagree, he knew that. He knew it and felt the pride of knowing if he wanted it, she would be his, she had chosen him. He was on his way to class, and he didn't want to stay and talk, but as he walked by the bench he casually dragged one finger across her shoulder blades, purposely sending a chill down her spine.

"Hey you. I'm off to class - see you later?"

Drue looked up. "Of course."

Quinn left, now he just had to decide if he wanted her.

Inside her she felt only panic. It had been a week, the feeling had passed. She didn't want to go anymore. She didn't need to go anymore. What was she supposed to say? And she had done this to herself. The idea haunted her, churning her stomach and blurring her vision. She had thrown herself into this lion's den and now she was forced to deal with it. What the hell had she been thinking? She had never had any help before, why was she set on it now? How would this solve her problems? She wasn't sick. She was fine. Life was good. What would she say? Does one just blurt something like that out? And what could the woman do anyway? Probably some stupid self-help spiel Drue could do herself, nothing her mom wouldn't have told her. And yet she had to go. What if she just skipped it? She had done that before, just quit and no one had noticed. But she knew she couldn't this time. That this time was different. She had to go, her friend knew her appointment was today and would check on her. But at that moment Drue would have done anything to not have to go.

The world slowly began to fade amidst her fear. Tears began to blur her vision; her legs were incapable of movement. The music in her room was as if from far away, unable to pull her back to reality. All she felt was a far off feeling of panic. Torture. Of growing doom. There was nothing left in her except these feelings. She knew now why she had originally asked to be taken. The short drive across town to the counselling center was to be the longest and hardest in her life. Her legs would barely move much less carry her to the destination for which she dreaded more than any other. But she knew she must go. If for no other reason then curiosity, she would get there.

Drue tried to make herself comfortable, a task that was virtually impossible given the circumstances. The office was a small square room with an odd display of not very peaceful pictures on the wall. The chair Drue sat in was a stiff backed chair that belonged in a classroom rather than a therapist's office. But, Drue reasoned, that is what you get when you go to a free clinic.

"So," the woman said, her pen poised over her notepad, "why are you here?"

"I cut," Drue said simply.

The woman was silent for a moment, and then she said, "ok." Just okay. Drue waited. The woman waited.

Drue looked out the window to the tree that was there, an oak tree, Drue guessed. She couldn't be sure. She was never very good at identifying plant life.

"So that's it?" The woman finally asked.

"Well yeah," Drue answered. She had thought that would be enough, she had thought that pretty much laid it all out there. "I want to be normal again," she added. The only elaboration she could think of.

"And what is normal?" The woman asked. She had brown hair. Short brown hair that fell about her face in a 50s style bob. She looked young. Drue tried to guess her age, thirty maybe?

Drue shrugged. "It means…. it means feeling again, it means not hating yourself so much you can't meet people's eyes, it means knowing sadness is okay, not believe God has forgotten about you."

The woman was silent for a moment, taking notes on her notepad. Drue wondered what she was writing. She wished she could read those notes. "And cutting does all these things for you?" The woman finally asked.

"Yes."

"How?"

Drue took a deep breath. She shifted her weight in an attempt to get more comfortable. "Well, cutting helps me feel because it is a tangible kind of pain, it gives me a secret so I can know something others don't and thus meet their eyes, it gives me a reason to cry, or not cry, depending on what I need. And it proves to God that I'm screwed up and he had better help me out. Plus, it serves as reminders, and helps me to remember and then eventually forget the people and things that hurt me. It grounds me."

Drue waited. She waited to hear how wrong what she did

was. She waited for the lecture.

Instead the woman just said, "those are all good reasons." Drue waited for the however. It never came. "I'm proud of you for finding such a good coping mechanism," the woman said.

Drue just stared at the woman dumbfounded. Proud? Proud! Was she kidding? That's not what she was supposed to say. She was suppose to yell at Drue, lecture her, tell Drue what she did was awful. Instead she said it was okay. Which is what Drue believed anyway. She had never understood the big deal of what she did. It was just a cut, it was just a scar. People got those all the times from natural causes. They always heal. She was never endangering her life. There were no long term effects. Surely no worse then any other bad habit, like biting her nails, or twirling her hair on her finger. Nothing she couldn't stop when life got just a little easier. She smiled to herself, yes, she should be proud of herself to be coping so well. After all, no one had offered to help her, so really she had done well. But then, why the heck was she in this uncomfortable chair, in this stifling office? "Yeah." Drue finally answered. "Thanks."

"Ok," the woman said then, "will I see you again next week?"

"Sure," Drue responded even though clearly there was no point.

Still she went each week and would sit for an hour in that small little office, curled up on an uncomfortable chair and talked to this woman. She wasn't bad this woman. Drue could tell she meant well, but it seemed to Drue she was a little scared. Why should the therapist be scared? Shouldn't that be my job? Drue wondered. But this woman seemed scared, unsure of herself, unsure of how to deal with Drue. Drue thought that was funny; the thought that perhaps this woman was scared of her.

Finally she gave in; just for a moment she let the tears come. She knew she didn't have a right to cry, she knew she was being stupid and that it was her own fault. But she cried anyway and then she reached for her razor because that's what she was used to doing when she cried. Then she stopped herself. She was supposed to be done with this. She looked next to her, where her writing sat neatly folded in a binder. She had written her last page, it was done, her story was done, she was supposed to be finished. You have told people you quit, she reminded herself, and yet.... She looked back to the razor. What else could save her right now? How else could she deal with this terrible aching inside?

"If I start I might not be able to quit again", she whispered the words trying to make herself believe them, she had to believe them. If she just got through the morning, then everything got easier. It was just this terrible first couple hours of every day that tortured her. But she didn't know if she could make it this day. The pain was too familiar, the setting, the desire, it was all just too much.

But then, despite the calling for it, despite the insistence pain that ached in her, despite the need, she made herself walk away.

A few minutes later, she walked back.

30

October 21st

….. we talked for maybe three minutes before he pulled my head towards his to kiss. At one point he asked me what I am thinking and I responded, "what the hell am I doing here?" and the strangest thing happened. My body went into panic. I've kissed guys since Roger but for some reason tonight was different, maybe because of Quinn, maybe because I've been thinking about Roger a lot recently. But all I could think of was, "bad," "wrong" "this is what starts depression" "you might get hurt" "you are finally getting better" "this is what starts all the bad stuff" all this from a kiss. A harmless kiss. When he pulled me on top of him I knew I couldn't do it anymore and said I had to leave. He, after all, had classes in the morning. I breathed better once I left.

I really thought I'd be okay, that casual dating would be fine. Hell this wasn't even that, it was just a random hook up. When I remind myself of that it's okay. But all I can think is how I might get hurt. Like what do I do if he does call or something? It made me so scared. Scared of things I didn't know existed in me. This fear of suffocation. I thought this is what I wanted, but I wasn't happy when I left tonight. So I don't know what will happen now. – Drue Potter

PS- I need to buy a razor.

Drue walked out of class to find her mom waiting for her.

"What are you doing here?" Drue asked. Drue was not sure whether to be happy, angry, worried, or just freaked out. She proceeded warily. She began walking to her next class, her mother followed.

"I was in the neighbourhood and thought maybe you'd like to do lunch today."

"I have class Mom."

"I know, but I can sign you out."

Drue stopped walking and looked at her mother. Was this really happening? Had her mother actually come all this way just to have lunch with Drue? Should she be suspicions? Her mom looked genuine enough, standing there in her favourite skirt and top looking at Drue expectantly. Drue glanced around at the crowded hall as kids pushed their way to class, at the giggling girls by the lockers and the guys that walked by too cool to say hello. It wasn't as if Drue wanted to be here anyway. She shrugged. "Okay."

Her mom smiled. They went to La Salsa, they ordered the same thing, and they sat on the tall chairs and talked about their lives.

The next day Drue got a voicemail from her mom. Just calling to say she had had a nice time the day before and would Drue like to have lunch again next week? Drue listened again and again to that message. Drue knew that her mother could never again play the role of Mom. Drue had lost her parents the moment that she called out for help and no one had come. Over the last year she had created a world in which she relied on no one. Her parents operated on the platform of; "you are almost eighteen, almost in college, we can't tell you what to do anymore." And Drue didn't ask. She just left at night for parties, and didn't bother explaining where she was going or what she did when she got there. But now, Drue realized, she could still have her parents as her friends. She didn't expect them to solve her problems, she didn't expect them to take care of her, she knew that was her job. But she could still ask advice, she could still share stories and they could still listen.

So the next week she did go out again with her mom. And they started going out for dinner together, all three of them on Sunday nights. Drue liked those nights best. She would finish her homework early and the three of them would go out someplace not too fancy and then come home and watch TV together. The world slowed down on those nights. Boys were forgotten, tests disappeared, Drue's problems could be put aside for the time being. It was nice. She felt safe.

That weekend she saw Quinn at a party. He smiled when he saw her and so she walked over.

"Hey."

"Hey."

"Want a drink?"

"What do you have?"

"Screw driver."

She grinned, "I'll have the same."

"You gonna try to keep up with me tonight?" He asked daring her.

She grinned back at him. "Without even trying."

But it did take trying. His tolerance was higher than hers, and so four drinks later her world was spinning. He kissed her then. She revelled in the prize at the end of the game, she had won. But just for a moment, then her head snapped back. As drunk as she was, she knew better than to kiss a boy with a girlfriend. "I thought you had a girlfriend," she accused.

He shook his head. "No. I did, not anymore."

She smiled, and leaned back into him. "Oh okay then." They

kissed again, and it didn't take long before he got up and extending a hand he pulled her up from the couch. Her body felt heavy and the world was just a little bit foggy on the corners, and yet she wanted to dance and laugh. Things were good. Life was good. She could almost see God wink at her as she followed Quinn into the bedroom. He hadn't forgotten her after all; God had just been waiting, saving the right person for her. Drue smiled to herself.

"What can I do to please you?" He asked. It was a whisper, a soft sound from another place and as the words came to her they made Drue blush and she shifted awkwardly. Quinn didn't notice, he kissed her lips and then moved quickly to her neck, her chest, her stomach. Drue giggled, and Quinn kissed her ear, "I want to make you happy," he whispered.

"You do," she whispered back.

He brushed a wisp of hair out of her eyes. "You are beautiful."

She smiled at him. "You aren't so bad yourself."

"Every guy at this party tonight wishes they were me right about now."

She laughed. "And every girl who has ever met you wishes they were me," she grinned. Then as the words sank in her head began to swim and she swallowed hard. She had just made a terrible mistake.

Drue had only one rule for hook-ups, but to keep that rule was to keep her sane, it was the only way she knew to protect her heart. She must never compliment a boy. He could compliment her all he wanted and she was to accept them with grace and love, but she was not to return the favour. Drue was incapable of lying or of not feeling and so a compliment could not be said without a strong belief behind it. And to see the true beauty in another, well that was to open your heart to that person and admit that you cared and allow the other person the power to do what they liked with that knowledge. The probability that they might do nothing, or worse might inflict pain, was just too great. Drue could not afford to set herself up for that kind of heartache. And so she was careful to never compliment a boy, she never allowed him to have that power over her, until now.

For as the words were spoken Drue opened her heart to this boy and she knew at that moment that she would be hurt.

That night she dreamt that after she kissed a boy there was blood. She thought it was from the act of hitting her head as she pulled away from him, but when she ran to the bathroom, and felt the back of her head the wet spot was at the base of her neck. She cleaned it and returned to the boy. They were sitting in the movie theatre when he tried to make another advance at her. She raised her elbow poised to dig into his ribs, "I will hurt you if you do" she said.

He looked at her, surprised, then scared, then angry, but he moved away. That was when she felt another wet spot on her back. She reached behind her and felt the blood. At first the feeling was panic. She got up and ran. She ran out of the theatre, and down the stairs which led to an even greater expanse of stairs, covered in snow and looking out upon a world that looked a bit like OZ only white instead of green.

There was a railing in the centre of the stairway separating those who were trudging up from those going down. She started scrambling down the steep stairs all the while feeling the blood coming from her back in several locations and coming from her mouth when she spat, a combination of blood and saliva.

"You should not leave," a man said on the other side of the railing, "once you leave it takes a very long time to get back."

She stared at him from the opposite side of the rail. He appeared to be neither coming nor going, just standing and watching those around him. "If you had not left," he told her, " I could have taken you to the nurse and fixed that for you."

She looked at him, and then down to the bottom of the stairs where the guard motioned for her to come down, a big grin on his face. She snuck under the railing and continued in the up line going once again into the walled city. Going up she was not so scared. The man disappeared, and as she walked she continued splitting blood and could feel it escaping her, but she was okay.

She saw those she loved then, standing at the top of the stairs. They looked at her with panic in their eyes, they were scared for her, but she was okay. She wanted to tell them this, explain that she was okay, she had accepted her fate, as she watched with comprehension but not fear as she lost what she knew to be a fatal amount of blood. And so a trail of blood followed her as she walked, a trail that had begun with a kiss from a boy.

Drue got her SAT scores back. She hadn't called in early like most of her friends. She was determined to not care that much. But she did care, she cared so much. She took the envelope into her room and looked at it. She remembered how it had felt to open her PSATs. The sinking feeling that had come when she read the score. The anger, the disappointment. She looked at her leg and saw that the F she had carved that day had faded. That was what last year had been for her, a failure. But this year, she hoped things were different this year.

She opened the envelope. It took her a moment to focus, her hands were shaking. When she did she breathed through her teeth, not quite believing what she read. But there it was: 1400. She had done it. She had done okay. She smiled to herself. Yes, she had done okay. It may not be the 1470 of her sister or best girlfriend, but it was enough. It was enough to get her out of here, and that was all that mattered.

A new girl started at work. She worked at night with Drue and Bryan. She watched Drue's eyes light up when Bryan walked in at the start of the shift. She watched as Bryan instantly walked up to Drue. She watched as the two stood together talking.

Later she walked up to Drue. "Is he your boyfriend?" She asked.

Drue's eyes went wide, "Bryan? Yes, Bryan's my boyfriend," she said sarcastically, then laughed, "no, we are just friends."

"Oh," the girl said, then added, "he's cute."

She walked away. Drue starred after her, Bryan? Cute? But Bryan had big eyes; he had flipped hair and wore collared shirts.

Drue laughed, Bryan was a prep. Then her smile faded, she watched as Bryan poured drinks at the bar, the way he laughed with customers, the way he winked at her when he caught her watching him. Drue smiled, kinda cute, Drue supposed, if you looked at him like that. It was just, well, it was Bryan. Still…. Drue laughed at herself. This was just what she needed - another boy!

Drue sat in that same uncomfortable chair, staring at the God forsaken oak tree, and the un-peaceful pictures on the wall. It had been three weeks.

"Now what?" She asked giving the woman a half smile as the words echoed in her head. Now what? Tell me how to fix my life, she wanted to scream. Because so far there was no fixing, so far there was only sadness. She sat calmly sitting and talking, the woman all the while unaware of how Drue's mind screamed at her, how her stomach turned and her body cried out at her weakness for being there. But Drue ignored all these things and sat and talked. She talked about her secrets, about the things she had never told anyone, had hardly admitted to herself. And the woman told her nothing.

She had a nice face, this woman, she looked kind, but Drue knew nothing about her. Didn't know if she had a family, or where she went when she wasn't sitting in the office. Hell, Drue didn't even know her last name. Yet this woman knew more about Drue than anyone in the world. It was funny how that worked. But, Drue reminded herself, this woman wasn't meant to be her friend, she wasn't meant to judge, she was meant to just listen…. like a journal. Drue smiled, yes she would think of this woman as a live journal. Just someone to hear the story Drue had wanted, for so long, to tell. This woman would hear that story. And maybe, Drue thought, if she thought of it like that then when she left it would be okay to be happy. It would be okay to leave the story in the office and return to life as it was meant to be.

"He sounds like a good guy, I don't understand why he didn't call."

"Yeah neither do I."

"I don't understand why he's being so terrible about this."

"I don't know, but damn I like him."

"I don't know Drue, he might not be worth it."

"The thing is I don't even really know him."

"Then how do you know that it is anything?"

"I don't, it's a dream."

"But what if he's not really this great guy you've made him out to be?"

"He might not be, but what if he is?"

"They usually aren't."

"Ah, but sometimes you get lucky. And then it's all worth it. He could be another Roger, he could be another dream come true."

"Dreams can be dangerous."

"The worst."

I won't cry. I won't let him make me cry. He doesn't deserve that. Is that why I'm even sad? Because of him? She had liked him for some time. She had broken her compliment rule for him - she shouldn't have done that - but why this devastation? Why this anguish? How pathetic was she? She hadn't had sex with this boy, she had kissed him, that didn't mean much in today's world, at least not to him, she knew that- every girl knew that. And she didn't regret it. She didn't wish she had done differently. She would do it again, if given the chance. But then why did she want to scream and cry and throw a fit like a little kid?

She looked in the mirror. She didn't look like a little kid. The girl that stared at her had traded her curly hair for straight, and her flower print tops for pink sheer spaghetti-straps. Her long earrings reached almost to her bare shoulders and her bangs covered one eye. No, the girl in the mirror was not a little girl at all. She was a sophisticated, put-together, young woman. Then why did Drue feel so much like a lost child? She felt like that little girl who, oh so long ago, gave her heart away to a boy. And though this time the boy was a one night stand instead of a boyfriend of eight months, the pain was similar, the tiredness, the anger, the longing to curl up in a ball and be taken care of. The girl in the mirror could handle this, the pettiness of wanting preferential treatment after one night, but Drue didn't know if she could. Drue took a deep breath, if that's what it was going to take she would just have to be that girl. And she could, outwardly she would smile, she would laugh, she would pretend nothing was wrong, but what would it cost her? What would she lose of herself?

Then Quinn did call. And he took her out to dinner. And Drue was happy.

31

November 1st

Uncontrollable shaking. That's what I've been reduced to. I don't know what's wrong with me, but something is DEFINITLY wrong. Wish I was sleeping more.

– Drue

Her sister came home for a visit. It was nice to be a family again, at least for a short time.

Then one night, her parents sat both daughters down and told them they were separating. Drue froze, the world went blank. "Just for a time, just to try it," her parents were saying, but Drue didn't hear them.

Stacey ran out of the room crying. Drue could hear her in the bathroom. She could also make out her parents, saying something about how Stacey was over-reacting; it wasn't that big a deal. Drue just sat, motionless, trying not to cry, trying not to think for fear that she might break down like Stacey. As always it was her sister who was allowed to fall apart while Drue was suppose to hold it together, so Drue just sat, because inside, she was numb.

When they were young Stacey used to throw ice around the kitchen when she got angry, crack, crack. Drue could remember the awful sound as it hit the cupboards and bounced across the room. She would cover her ears and try to block it out, but still she could hear it. Crack, crack. The incessant sound of ice breaking. That is what she heard now. As her parents stood there calmly, bewildered by the fuss their news had caused, Drue heard the pelting of ice in her head. The world tilted dangerously. Her head pounded with the cracking.

The lake that she had been so delicately treading on had at last shattered and as she fell into the icy water she wondered if she could breathe amongst the floating glaciers - all that was left of her perfect family unit - separate pieces of ice. What did it matter if they were all in the same lake? They were all just broken pieces now. Drue thought she might be sick.

She sat. The silence engulfed her and she sat. It was one of those rare moments in life where she had nothing to say, even to herself. Her heart raced, her stomach clenched, but inside her head there was, nothing. Just tiredness, blankness. The confusion had so blurred her vision she could no longer read her own thoughts.

So she sat. The silence engulfed her but did not calm her. She still hurt too much inside. I asked her how she managed to just sit for nine hours. She did not tell me. She did not say how for what felt like forever she had laid curled in a ball in tears unable to move, unable to control the sobs that escaped her. She could not explain these tears, nor could she explain what it took to recover from such tears. And that was why she sat. The music played, the computer ran, but Drue just sat. And the silence engulfed her because within her there was nothing.

Drue wasn't eating. On good days she would make it to class, but even as her body sat in the classroom her mind remained far away fighting against the icy water threatening to freeze her. She could not function without the stability she had known as her family. She would find herself standing in a room of friends unable to recognize a face or find tears rolling down her cheeks for no reason at all.

Still, she fought the urge to cut. She let her razor sit in her drawer pristine and new. Drue could not even find the power in herself to fix this problem; this one was up to God.

It didn't take long for Drue to give up on counselling. It was easier than she thought too, she just stopped going. The women called once, but when Drue didn't call back, there was nothing more. They forgot her just like that. She didn't understand how even after she told people they were so willing to let her walk away, but they were. The world was funny like that.

She began to spend most of her time at her friend's house. This way her parents didn't know if she was eating, if she was going to class, and she didn't have to bear the idea that if she went home her mom wouldn't be there. As it turned out her friend also had a small nook in the closet for which Drue acquired a great affinity. I came over to visit one day and this is where I found her, curled up in the closet in a tight ball.

"What are you doing? "She looked at me and just shrugged. "Drue you have to come out. You have to get your life back."

"I like the smallness. I like that I can't sit up straight, and I can't straighten out my legs. It's comforting. Like being held," she said in a barely audible whisper.

"Drue please," I begged. But she just stared at me her eyes blank.

Quinn got her out. Not because of anything he did, but

because she didn't want him to know she was hurt. So when he called, at first she didn't talk to him, but then eventually she did. And when he told her she was missed at Friday night parties, she said she'd go, and she went. She would plant that smile on her face and she would laugh and he would tease her and they would kiss. And for a little while at least she would forget. She would drink then and have to be helped home. But slowly she did get better; she began to show up at school again, she began to return to her lunches with her mom, she began to work on her college applications. Life began to return to normal.

"I saw Quinn today," she cooed to her friend.

Her friend laughed. "That's good Drue."

Drue smiled. The foolish smile, that spread from ear to ear and she couldn't control. The smile that made her cover her mouth with her hands in embarrassment. "I know isn't it" she said in a small voice never breaking her smile.

"You like him so much."

Drue covered her face in her hands, and laughed, "I know.... It's so bad!"

It was a weird feeling, neither unpleasant nor unfamiliar but un-present in her life for so long now that she had begun to doubt if she could feel it again. The butterflies, the uncontrollable smile. She looked at him. She wished she could hold his hand or brush that wisp of hair from his face. But she couldn't, so she just smiled. Yes, she remembered this feeling. She remembered the joy of a single compliment and the agony of being forgotten, but unlike the last time when she fought these feelings, now she embraced them. She tucked both joy and agony deep in her heart and let herself feel. For these were the aspects missing in her life. Though she knew no good could come of it, she smiled because her life was as it should be once again. The cute boy with his dancing eyes and contagious smile. This boy held the traces of a someone long ago and he filled her life of its broken and missing pieces. She did not care what others said about him, or even of the things she told herself. For there was his smile, there were his eyes and all she could think of was how she wanted to kiss those lips, how she wished to be the cause of just a little of the joy behind those eyes. When all was said and done just having him in the same room as her, just being allowed to be near him brought her a joy she hadn't felt in a long time. A joy that extended from the tips of her toes to the edges of her smile. A joy that made her feel like a little kid again. And she missed the boy from long ago, missed the childhood he had stolen from her. But then her mind would flick to the boy across the room and for just a minute, before her conscious could take over, she allowed herself to dream of this boy giving that childhood back to her. She wondered, just for that quick moment what it would be like to have this boy in her life for awhile. But then her mind took over and the thought was gone. After all, she knew better than to expect. So she just smiled and returned to her book. After all, he would still be there tomorrow and for now, that was all that mattered.

32

December 13th

Dear Scarlette,

So Thanksgiving has come and gone. I suppose it's telling how little I write, telling of what I'm not sure, but certainly telling. Maybe that I don't think about my life. I do everything I can to just feel and act, no thinking, or questioning, or evaluating.

So yeah Thanksgiving. It was nice to see Stacey. The one good thing to come out of all Mom and Dad's problems is that Stacey and I have gotten a lot closer. I don't like that we always have to have a big family meeting before Stacey leaves - it leaves me feeling icky. I hope we don't have to have them over Christmas break too.

I'm ready to be in love. It has taken me some random hook ups to get here, but I think I'm there. I think it's partly because of Mom and Dad. I need someone there for me since they aren't. I want to believe in love again. Too bad I haven't met anyone yet. It'd be a lot easier if I liked someone who liked me. Hmmmm….

Oh and I didn't write my paper. I tried, but it just didn't work, the other problem with all this Mom and Dad stuff - I can't concentrate! I wrote my professor begging family emergency, hopefully I'll get an extension otherwise I'll be up VERY late tonight. I don't know that I'm doing very well in any of my classes. It's hard for me to concentrate. I need distractions to keep me happy so doing work all the time is tough. I should start my paper.

- Drue

"No one ever gets back together after a trial separation, do they?"

"I dunno," I answered, "if ever there were two people to be the exception, it'd be your parents."

She sat on my bed her back against the wall so that her legs stuck out off the edge. Unable to bend them it gave the distinct impression of a four year old in a diner booth, she bounced her legs up and down increasing the likeness. "I don't know about that," she said thoughtfully, "I used to think we were this grand exception, the perfect family in a sea of corruption. But now we are just as dysfunctional as every other family."

I shook my head. "Nah, your family is still special Drue." She raised here eyebrows at me. "Not that kind of special. Just, I think your parents' relationship is stronger than you give it credit for."

"You haven't been living in that house for the last year. God Chris, it's awful."

"Then, isn't this for the best? I mean, don't you want your parents to be happy?"

"Maybe, but it's certainly making me much more miserable. Oh and then there's my sister who keeps wanting to have these heart to hearts about how this is making us feel. As if talking about how much it sucks will make it go away. Uh, I'm really ready to go to college." She took my pillow and hugging it to her chest let herself fall over on the bed.

"You know Drue, running away doesn't actually solve anything."

She sat up abruptly and looked me in the eye. "Of course it does. Once I'm out of the house, or better yet the state, what the hell will I care what my parents do?"

"Because you of all people know you are inexplicably linked with your parents and that no matter where you are in the world you will be affected by the state of affairs in your family. I'm sorry Drue, it's just true."

Drue stared at me blankly for a long time. "God I hate when you are right!" She said at last falling over once more onto my bed.

I just smiled. "Has to happen on occasion."

She glared at me. "So long as you don't make a habit of it."

I smiled. "I'll try not to". Then I leaned over and picked up the DVD that sat next to me on my desk, I hold it up for Drue's inspection, "*Friends*?" I asked.

Her face lit up. "Please."

I put on the show and for the time being all other things were forgotten in favour of the mindless humour of television.

Drue got to go home early from work. She was pleased; she wanted to go out with her friends and thought she could just make it. She walked into the kitchen to say goodbye. The cooks gave her a quick wave, the other waitress a simple, "see you next week."

Bryan was loading glasses into the dishwasher; he looked up from what he was doing. "You can't go," he said.

She smiled, by now she was used to his teasing. "You'll be just fine," she said reassuringly.

"No I'm serious, you can't leave. I need you," he said, his face completely straight, his voice serious.

Drue rolled her eyes no longer sure if he was teasing - what was he saying? "Sorry," she said with a shrug and a smile. She left. She got out to her car, turned it on and began driving home. What could he have possibly meant by that? What was going on with him? He was just teasing, it's what he did. He teased with all the wait staff; he would have said that to anyone, right?

Twenty minutes later she drove back. She walked into the kitchen. Bryan was now at the counter talking to the cooks, he smiled when he saw her. "Come back to work some more?"

Drue smiled. "Yeah, I thought, hey now that I've had a twenty minute break, I'll just go back." She laughed and shook her head, "nah, I forgot my sunglasses."

"Is that all it's been?" He asked glancing at the clock.

"Yep, twenty minutes. I know, it feels like forever when I'm not here," she teased.

"It's true." He said simply.

Drue grinned "I understand, it's just not the same without me but you are just going to have to make do." And she walked out, for the second time that night a grin on her face, but with no better idea of what Bryan was talking about. What did he really think of her?

There are promises you make to yourself. Promises that only you can know about and only you can keep. She made one such promise. She promised she would have no regrets. It started with him, way back then; when taking chances meant calling him, or going up to him at lunch. Now things weren't as simple, now taking chances meant kissing a boy, it meant taking your clothes off, it meant giving away a little piece of yourself. These chances weren't as easy to take. Sometimes these chances hurt her. She wondered if she regretted it. Did she regret loving him? Was all the pain worth it? She always had to answer yes. But the pain was always there. The hurt and sadness, but regret? No, never regret. She would give her heart even when she knew she shouldn't, and in return she got a perfect night here, a perfect night there, and in-between she would cry. In-between she would feel alone. But those nights, those times she took the chance, those times were magical.

The night started off beautifully. It was New Years, she was dressed up and she was ready to have fun. She went with Quinn to a party and when she walked in she was delighted to find she knew almost everyone there. She looked hot and she knew it. She could tell in the way Quinn had looked at her when he had opened the door for her that night and she could see it in the way the other guys looked at her as she walked into the room. She also knew that she was the envy of every girl in the room because she was with Quinn, who was undoubtedly one of the most attractive people at the party. She smiled to herself, yes tonight was going to be perfect.

Quinn brought her a drink, she finished it quickly. She drank another and another. It was more than she had ever drank in her life, but she loved it. The world spun and the edges of her vision blurred, but still she laughed and danced. She played beer pong with a friend, they won and she was delighted. She laughed so much that night.

But then things began to go wrong. A person whom she thought was her friend came up to her. "Hey babe."

She turned and grinned at him. "Hello darlin'. How are you?"

He smiled back at her. "I 'm good. You wanna go talk?"

She shrugged lightly. "Okay. I have to wait my turn for the next game anyway. James, I'll be right back, k?" She called to her partner. He gave her a wave and she skipped off. Her friend followed. When they were outside she turned to him, "so what's up?"

"I'm worried about you," he said.

Drue furrowed her brow. "Why would you be worried about me?"

"I think Quinn is just using you," he said bluntly.

Drue's eyes went wide. "What do you mean?"

Her friend remained calm. "I just don't think it's anything serious for him. He just got out of this relationship. I think you are a rebound. You need to be careful that's all. I don't want to see you get hurt."

Drue stared at him, not saying a word. It never occurred to her to second-guess this friend. She saw no reason to distrust this older, and thus presumably wiser, person. Not to mention Drue was drunk, she wasn't thinking of this person's ulterior motives, it didn't occur to Drue to get angry with this person, or to blame him, instead she just got scared. "He's not using me," she responded shaking her head, trying to put the idea out of her head. "He's not," she repeated.

"He is," her friend responded. It was said with kindness, but Drue couldn't understand why she had to hear this. Why now?

In a different situation Drue may have thought about this, agonized over it, rehashed it, but at that moment there was no thinking going on. Instead she stormed inside to look for Quinn. He was in the far corner talking to friend. She walked up to him. "Are you just using me?"

His eyes went wide and he stared at her, "Drue what are you talking about?"

"You heard me, the question is simple enough," she said, her voice rising.

Quinn took her shoulders and steered her away, giving an apologetic glance to his friend who had stopped mid-sentence.

They reached an empty room and Quinn, still holding Drue's shoulders, looked her in the eye. "Now, what is going on?" He asked her calmly.

Drue's voice dropped to an appropriate level, she put her arms on his shoulders. "Are you just using me? Like what are we? What are you doing with me?"

"I don't know," was all he said. It was a fair answer, it was probably the truth. But it was not what Drue wanted to hear. She wanted him to declare his love for her; she wanted to know that once again she had found her prince charming. She wanted to know he cared. He wasn't willing to lie to her.

She stared at him dumbly. "That's it. You don't care at all?"

"I didn't say that Drue. I said, don't assume anything. I'm still figuring it all out."

Drue turned and ran. She ran upstairs and into an empty

bedroom where she sank to the floor in tears. Maybe if she hadn't been drunk, maybe if she hadn't already been suffering from depression, maybe if she hadn't pinned so many hopes on him. But she had. And so with those words her world fell on top of her. The alcohol, still so much in her system, left Drue helpless. She could not use reason; she could not use logic, there was nothing. She began to talk to herself, a helpless mumbling of nothings to try to calm herself down. None worked. It took her only about five minutes to realize what she needed. She began to search the room for something sharp.

It provided nothing.

She went downstairs with the thought of going to the kitchen to get a knife, but as she came upon the landing Quinn was there and instead of making it to the kitchen she collapsed into him sobbing uncontrollably. Somehow it all came out then, that she was on her way to the kitchen to find a knife, that she cut, that she was hurting so much. He held her and stroked her head, but he refused to comfort her, he refused to let her cry or to tell her it would be okay. Instead for the first time in her life she was reprimanded.

"How can you possibly think that you have problems?" He asked her.

"But my parents," she sobbed, "and my sister, and school, and..."

"And what Drue? Your parents are alive and loving and you can always go home. Your sister still loves and misses you, you are brilliant, you'll get in wherever you want and you'll be able to afford it. Are you so weak that you can't deal with these minor things? That because of a B on an exam, or because your parents, both of whom love you so much, aren't living together, you feel you have the right feel sorry for yourself?" She stopped crying, she stared at him, he continued, "How can you be so weak, so selfish? You want to hear hardship? My dad left three years ago, my mom is sick, and so though I wanted to move out I have to stay home to take care of my younger siblings. I got into NYU, but we couldn't afford it so I'm at City College and working two jobs so that *maybe* in a few years I'll be able to get out of this town. But still I get up every day without cutting, without pitying myself, without begging depression. So don't give me any of your sob stories because they are nothing compared to what I've seen. You are damn lucky Drue Potter and it's about time you realised that instead of just feeling sorry for yourself."

Drue was stunned. She shook but no tears came, she was speechless. Never before had she been scolded for her problem, never had she been told to suck it up and grow up. She had wanted to be lectured for the last year and a half and no one had. Now tonight, when all she wanted was a hand to hold, and a hug to comfort her, the lecture came. The pain didn't go away, the breathing didn't become easier. And when the tears began again they just worsened. She clung to him, but he continued to tell her about his struggles, about how this world wasn't going to pity her and how she had to fix this. Eventually when she realized she couldn't take it anymore she got up and left. She just said goodbye and he got up and left without offering to drive her home, without so much as a backwards glance.

She knew then that it was over. Just like that. She had lost him. She had screwed up the best thing in her life, the one thing that was getting her up in the morning. Because of her stupid addiction she had lost everything.

She dragged herself to the bathroom and sank to the floor. The tile was cold against her skin and in the mirror she could see her face smudged with tears and dirty with makeup. She could hear the laughter in the other room, the yelling as the countdown began. She began to sober up and her head began to pound. The world was on its side now and she clung onto the counter for dear life, half scared, half hoping that she would in fact simply fall off the earth as it spun about on its tilted axis. She talked to herself, she tried to calm herself, but there was no calmness to be found. She was done. She had lost everything. There was nothing for her to wake up to the next morning. She decided then that there was only one thing to do.

She tore open the bathroom cabinets looking for any pills she could find. The bathroom, obviously that of a boy college student, was nearly empty save one bottle of aspirin. She poured the bottle out onto the tile floor which made a satisfying ping as each pill hit the cold surface. One by one she took the pills. There were not many, but she hoped they would be enough. Just enough so that she would never have to wake up again. Quinn was right, she was weak. She was unappreciative and selfish. She crawled to a bedroom and into the bed she found there. Pulling the covers up over her chin, she hoped that when she fell to sleep that night, she would never wake up again. That was her only prayer.

She did wake up the next morning. And after a bit of a struggle she got herself out of bed, planted a smile on her face and made it through the day. Then she made it through the next day, and the next, each a little easier. His words stayed with her.

33

January 24th

Dear *Scarlette,*

I'm 18. Have been for two and a half weeks and I don't feel any older. Or wiser. Or anything. Shouldn't I? Shouldn't I all of a sudden FEEL different, now that I'm an adult. I gave it a few weeks just to see if it was a delayed reaction sort of thing, it's not. I remember when I turned 13 I did the same thing. Waiting, to feel difference. But I did, then. I mean, it took 48 hours, but then all of a sudden all those awful burdens of being a teenager fell upon me in full force. And it was as if I never could remember a time when I didn't spend nights crying myself to sleep or waking up sad for no reason. I just, well, felt DIFFERENT. But now? No change. No more mature or older at all. I could be sixteen still. I wonder if I'll ever feel grown up.

Love, Drue Potter

Two weeks later Drue saw Quinn at a party. He was there looking his usual laid back self and her body called out to him. Just for a second, just for a moment, but it was enough. When she saw him leave she followed. He was upstairs. He was looking for something in a drawer, she sat down on the bed.

"Quinn?"

He turned, smiled. "Drue."

"Can we talk for a second?"

"Sure," he came and sat down next to her.

"Quinn, I'm sorry." Drue looked at her hands. Quinn didn't say anything so Drue continued, "do you think you'd ever give me a second chance?"

Quinn was quiet for a moment, and Drue didn't dare say another word. "I learned a lot about you… fast," he said, but then he smiled and his eyes got that familiar dancing look in them, "but you are hot."

She smiled. "So, maybe?"

He gave a short nod. "Yeah."

"Okay." Drue said then, "I can live with that."

And she left, unsure of what they had just decided.

Later that night, Drue watched as Quinn left with another girl. It was impossible to know whether they left to smoke or hook up, but after thirty minutes Drue knew even if it had started as the former it was no longer the case. Well, she thought stubbornly, two can play that game. She took another beer from the fridge.

Just then Bryan walked in the door. She drew back in surprise and then smiled, "Bryan!"

He smiled when he saw her. That was all it took. She had decided who she was going to hook up with that night.

The next night when neither boy appeared Drue found a new boy. Drue liked flirting; she liked the game of it. It made her feel pretty and it helped convince her she didn't miss Quinn, but she did. And when she actually won the boy, when she got him to kiss her, well then she quickly lost interest. She thought she wanted to fall in love, that that was what she was looking for, but Drue hardly knew what love was anymore. She certainly didn't know trust, or loyalty, or consistency. She relied only on herself, and she hated herself.

Quinn's words would be the thing she would hear every morning as she opened her eyes, those words telling her she was weak, spoiled and ungrateful. It was those words that pushed her to be better. She threw herself into her school work, into her exercises, into everything she could so that she could prove him wrong. She threw out her razors and meant it this time. She wasn't going to go back.

Drue walked into work hesitantly. She hadn't seen Bryan since the party the week before and she was nervous. Would it be weird? Awkward? Would they still remain friends? She spotted him almost instantly. He turned and met her eyes, he smiled. "Hey girl," he said walking over.

"Hey." She returned his smile.

"Good to see you are on staff tonight." She just raised her eyebrows. "How's your weekend going?"

She shrugged. "Fine. Went to a party at Barry's last night. Missed you."

"Yeah, I was in San Diego."

"Oh how was that?"

"Really fun. Just went for a few days to see a friend from High School."

"Very nice."

"Yeah. So I was thinking we should chill at some point this week."

Drue smiled. "Definitely, but when were you thinking? Because tomorrow night I have loads of homework."

"Well how about Monday or Tuesday?"

She nodded. "Ok, anything in particular?"

"I'm not one for planning ahead much. What do you wanna do?"

"Oh I dunno. Just curious if you were thinking something specific."

"We could do dinner of some sort or something like that, for conventional purposes."

Drue raised her eyebrows. "Conventional purposes?"

Bryan smiled. "Yeah. Convention."

Drue shrugged. "Ok. Give me a call later?"

"Definitely will. I should probably get to the bar now," he said looking over his shoulder as guests began arriving.

"Yeah that's probably a good idea," she said smiling as she watched him leave.

It was two and a half weeks and six parties later that Drue realized Quinn wasn't coming back. She sat in her room and stared at nothing. He hadn't called. He had said he'd call and he hadn't called. She knew that meant he was avoiding her, that he didn't care, that she had lost him. And that hurt. It hurt as deep as a hurt can go, and she wanted so much to find her razor. She wanted to have that mark on her arm, she wanted the relics, she wanted God to notice and to help her. She wanted to remember him. But she also remembered his words and she had made it four months, that was longer than she had ever gone before. She had lost him to gain this passage over the two month bridge and she wasn't going to waste it. She couldn't give up now. And so she just sat and cried because she didn't know what else to do. She didn't know how to fight this. She didn't know how to be her own inspiration; she had never done this before. But she knew that she would have to start.

Then the withdrawals began. Like clockwork as each two months came so did the normal symptoms. Dark clouds formed over a normal life. The restlessness returned to make her daily routine seem like something she hated, food became her enemy and in class she never seemed to have the right answer. At night she would cry for Roger and the comfort of the past. She fought it. She made herself climb out of bed every day.

Then the attacks started. In full force she would be sitting in her room and all of a sudden the room would blur and she would have trouble breathing. She would fall to the floor and rock herself back and forth, back and forth, slowly until the moment passed. Sometimes it would last only seconds, other times she would sit rocking for twenty minutes. Sometimes the attacks wouldn't come for weeks, other times they would happen more than once a day. Each time she would play Quinn's voice in her head, the voice that told her to stop, the boy that reminded her what she was fighting so hard for. The problem was he was no longer there, so she found herself fighting alone.

"Come on Drue, lighten up."

She was drunk, he was drunker. He was leaning against a wall to hold himself up and she stood in front of him. His name was Scott. She had hooked up with him once, he was cute that night. They had flirted and she had liked the game. She had gone home with him instead of calling Bryan for a ride. But that wasn't the case tonight. Tonight she just wanted to go home and sleep and he just seemed like a drunk.

"No," she responded.

"Why? What are you afraid of?"

"I'm not afraid of anything. I just don't want to go."

"Grow up Drue. Graduation is in two months, then it's college, you can't live like a prude in college."

Drue just glared at him. "Fuck you."

"Exactly. Let's go."

Drue's jaw dropped. "I can't believe you just said that."

"Why?"

"Because... because you know that's not what I meant." Drue was angry beyond words. How dare this boy make her feel bad for who she was, for what she believed?

"Come on Drue, at least take a shower with me. That's all. A harmless shower."

She raised her eyebrows. "You go take a shower, I'm going home."

"You are a bitch you know that."

"Because I wouldn't go and take a shower with you at some stranger's house?"

"Because I was having a perfectly good night until you went and got all uppity on me."

"This is crap. Call me when you aren't drunk and want to hang out," Drue said turning to leave. She could feel the tears in the back of her eyes.

"I have. It's your turn now."

Drue turned back to the boy. She wondered if he really had called, if somehow she had not noticed that he actually cared. Then she sighed and shook her head. "Well this conversation is not going to make me want to call you any more."

"I just want to have a little fun. You do too, you are just being lame."

"How do you know what I want? Because frankly what I would like is to go home."

"That's not true and you know it. You are just being lame about it."

"Maybe I like being lame."

"Well you shouldn't. No one likes hanging out with someone who is a prude and lame."

"Good bye Scott." Drue turned and walked outside.

She leaned against the wall and took a deep breath of fresh air trying to steady her pounding heart. Was she lame? Was she pathetic? Was she somehow working against the cosmic plan for eighteen year olds? She sighed, probably. Just another way she was letting someone down. She let herself slide down the wall feeling the brick against her back. The world was fuzzy from drink and her eyes were heavy. She wondered how she would get home. She wished she was in bed. She wished she had someone to call. She wished she didn't feel so alone.

She was soon functioning as if under water. Unable to pull herself back to reality with a cut, she eventually had an attack from which she never woke up. She could breathe, and she could see, but she functioned always on the verge of tears, the slightest thing setting her off. She couldn't quite put two and two together, never seeing those things right in front of her, whether it was the homework problem she struggled over or a friend extending a hand of love. Instead, she slept less and drank more and tried to not think of the cloud in her head.

However, the cloud remained and Drue continued to live in her dream world unsure of what or who she was. Some days she'd wake up and be a mature twenty five year old ready to conquer the world, other days she was a child scared of all things unknown, other days she was a teenager angry at the world, some days she loved herself and laughed, teased and flirted, other days she'd hate herself so deeply that she hated those who were kind to her. On the best of days she was no one at all, for on those days she would only sleep, blowing off work and class, she would lie in bed, listen to her stomach churn and wonder if she was getting skinner. She wondered if she'd ever be thin again. She would go days without eating, go weeks on just liquids, she once tried to make herself throw up, but when that didn't work, she simply cursed herself instead. Still, it was no good, the self hatred lay deep inside, the only fire left.

34

March 21st

Scarlette,

I talked to Roger today, for the first time in who knows how long. It was really nice. I miss him. I miss him as a friend, as the guy who could always make me laugh. I think though, that I'm totally over him as anything else. But it was nice to talk to him, however brief. I'd forgotten how much I enjoy his company. I miss his presence in my life, but I don't understand how he could have seemed so important. Oh shit, dinner. Gotta run.

Love, Drue

I had lost Drue. I wandered about the rooms, poking my head through doorways, smiling apologetically as I interrupted various act of promiscuity and illegality. At last I came down the outdoor stairs and found Drue there. She was leaning against the back of the house a cigarette idly burning down in one hand while she stared blankly in front of her. It took me a moment to realize she was crying. "Drue?" She turned to face me: dark circles framing her bloodshot eyes. "You okay?" Her head gave a small tilt, presumably a nod. She took a drag from the cigarette breathing in deeply and exhaling slowly. "Since when did you begin to smoke?" She shrugged looking away from me back to her spot in the distance. "That is a cigarette right?" Again a slight shrug showed me at least she heard. "Drue" I let my voice fade off.

"I think I'd like to try 'E'" she said softly as if making the decision to herself, rather than me. "I heard it makes you happy." Her voice was flat, expressionless.

"But Drue, why?"

She didn't look at me, just took a piece of paper from her back pocket and handed it to me. I took it from her and squinted at the writing in the dim light of the outdoor patio. University of California Berkley was embossed on the top of the page. I began to read, "Ms. Potter, We are pleased to offer you acceptance…" I looked up at Drue. She was staring off into the distance her hand raised holding the cigarette, which was now close to burning her fingers, inches from her face.

"Drue that's…." she gave a small shake of her head. I stopped. Then I understood. This was good, the letter from BU the day before was even better, for it meant Drue could get out of California, but it didn't mean anything, not really for there would be no letters from Stanford, or Harvard, or even Princeton, or Brown. Drue had not applied to any ivy leagues. She had said it was because she wouldn't want to go to any of those schools even if she did get in, but in truth it was because she was too scared. Drue didn't know if she could handle the rejection. In theory, she'd be fine, but if she had actually received the rejection letter from Stanford, well then she would have had proof that she wasn't as good as her sister. That even though all these years she told herself she was just as smart, she'd have physical evidence that that wasn't the case. So she had applied to schools that she thought she could get in. And she did. But there was no dream behind any of them. She had, after all, given up on dreams.

I sighed handing her back the paper. She took it numbly. "Come on, let's get you home." I took her hand and she let me lead her to the car.

"You have to do more," Bryan told her, "I do stuff for you and at some point I expect reciprocation."

She began to cry. He took her hand. He hadn't meant to make her cry. He was just trying to be honest, talk to her like an adult.

The problem was Drue wasn't an adult. She was eighteen years old, but that night she felt about fifteen. All she wanted to do was kiss. Everything else scared her. Maybe one day. But not now, not tonight.

And though she wanted to, she didn't know how to explain. She knew she loved this boy, but she knew she was disappointing him. She knew that she was still too broken to be able to handle him. This boy who was so sure of himself, so sure of life, who had been through so much and yet still loved life for its simplicities. She didn't even know who she was anymore, much less how she fit into the universe.

Sometimes when she woke up to play the right part they would spend amazing nights together, arguing about music, taking walks on the beach, or dancing to terrible music at a party, but other days she didn't want that life and she would miss Roger or be angry for what she lost in Quinn. And he scared her, this boy who was a reality like none of the others in her life had been. He was not the idealized dream of Roger or Quinn, or the one night hook up of so many boys before. He challenged her, he forced her to take responsibility for her actions, he forced her to grow up, he treated her as an equal, he refused to take care of her. And yet he did these things while still supporting her, not asking that she be perfect, but still asking more than she had to give. He didn't realize she was broken. He didn't understand that she was incapable of looking at her life with the clarity with which he did his. When Drue looked at her life all she saw was the water from her tears, the water that was slowly drowning her. But she knew in her inability to explain this she was disappointing him. She could see it in his eyes. And so she cried.

Drue curled her legs up on the bed, she hid her face in her hands. "Drue." He pulled her hands from her face, "Drue talk to me." He sat up next to her, watching her intently. She could only shake her head, a tear rolled down her cheek. She wished she didn't have to disappoint him. She wanted so much to be that person he saw in her. "It's just a matter of wanting to give your partner pleasure." He tried to explain.

More tears. Drue didn't want pleasure, she wanted comfort. She wanted hugs and someone to tell her it'd be better tomorrow. So though she wished she could provide Bryan with everything that night the thought of doing anything other than lie there gaining support from human closeness seemed unthinkable.

Drue got up, "I need to go home."

"Wait, Drue."

But she was gone.

Two nights later Drue woke up twenty. She met Bryan at a party, they drank, they messed around. It was good. Two days later however they were having the same conversation. Drue began to get anxious at the thought of going to Bryan's. What would tonight bring? Would she be okay? Would she disappoint him? She began to find reason's not to go home with him. She'd spend time in the party with him, and then go to a friend's house to sleep. But on those nights Drue would miss him. Miss his arms as they held her close, miss hearing about his day, miss seeing his face when she woke up in the morning.

She was so tired of being broken.

It was raining outside so I didn't hear the car pull up. But I heard the doorbell as it sounded through our house and I remember thinking it odd that my parents had invited someone over this late. I went to open the door.

She was crying. I stood silently, wondering what to do. She hadn't told me she was coming over. She stood on the doorstep, tears running down her face and droplets of rain falling from her hair. She wore the sweatshirt I had given her. It was too big, her hands were lost beneath the sleeves, but as she reached up to wipe her eyes, she did not bother to uncover her hands. Her hair was thrown up in a messy bun on the top of her head, random curls falling about her face haphazardly. Her pyjama bottoms dragged on the ground, the bottoms dirty from where she had walked through a puddle, and despite the rain and cold outside she wore only flip flops on her feet. Her eyes were wide, begging me for something, but I didn't know what. I opened the door a little wider, "Want to come in?" She gave a small nod and took a step forward. The tears continued in a steady stream and she brushed them away as she followed me down the hall to my room. She sat on my bed. I sat in my chair. I looked at her. She still had not said a word.

We sat in silence.

I got up and got her a glass of water. She took it from me with both her hands and held it lovingly in front of her.

"What's wrong?" I finally asked. Drue was never silent. She said what she thought and she was always thinking something. And I didn't know, if when she started to speak, she would be screaming or crying. It scared me, not knowing.

But this night she didn't say a word. In response to my question she just sat and stared past me. The tears continued, but she didn't even try to brush them away anymore.

"Drue, please." It was a beg, a plea. She had forgotten I was there. All her focus lay in a spot over my shoulder. Finally her eyes came back to me. She looked down at her lap and the water she still held so tightly. She set it down. Then without a word, she rolled up her sleeves for me to see. Across both her wrists were two dark lines. I stared at them and swallowed hard. Then I looked back up at her face.

She rolled her sleeves back down and met my gaze. Her voice when she spoke at last was small, "I really tried not to," she shook her head. "I'm just not strong enough, Chris."

I just sat. I wanted to take it from her. I wanted to take this pain that was etched on her face away from her, but I didn't know how. I didn't know how to give her that strength or to make things right. So I did nothing.

She curled up her legs and hugged them to her chest. "What am I going to do if I can't beat this Chris? I want to be better. I really do." She buried her face in her knees.

I didn't ask why she did it. I didn't ask what prompted this relapse, because I knew it didn't matter. Not at this point, not in this moment. I came over and sat beside her. I took her hand in mine. She didn't look up, she didn't acknowledge my presence, but she let me take her hand, and so I held it. We sat in silence while the rain came down outside. Eventually her breathing slowed. She leaned against me, "I think they are crying for me", she said. It was a whisper, and I wondered if I had imagined the words. I stroked her head.

"Yes, yes they are," I whispered back at last. Then we just sat listening to the rain. There was nothing else to do.

Drue asked him on the phone. She knew it was the easy way out, but the idea of asking him in person made her stomach do turns and her hands shake. At least on the phone he couldn't see these visible signs of her nerves. "Will you go to prom with me?"

"I would love to." The answer was almost instantaneous. Drue smiled.

Then there was silence. What did you say after you asked? She hadn't thought about that part. Then she heard Bryan's voice, "when is it?"

"Ummmm." Drue ran to her calendar. "Next month, the 18th."

"Damn," the curse was quiet but unmistakable. Drue's heart dropped. "What do you have?"

Bryan sighed, "I'm going to be in New York that weekend."

"And there is no way you can just not go?"

"Drue."

"I know, I know."

"I'm sorry."

"Yeah me too."

"I really wanted to go."

"I know."

Her parents moved back in together. It was an occurrence that shocked Drue almost as much as their separation. She had gotten accustomed to avoiding her home, sleeping at friend's houses, or flirting with a boy until he offered her a bed. Now she would return home to find her parents smiling, laughing, teasing. There were still nights when they would stay up late talking and Drue would find herself sneaking out and walking the few blocks to her friend's house. But home was no longer a place to be avoided at all costs; it slowly was becoming that place of comfort once more. Drue found she had missed her bed, her room, missed dinners with her parents. She discovered she liked her parents, that they made her laugh, they told good stories and they listened when she talked. She still couldn't trust them like she use to, but then, Drue didn't trust anyone like she use to.

"I'm not going to Prom."

"Chris you have to go."

"I hate dances."

"So, it's Prom for God's sake. You have to go."

"No, I…"

"Shit."

"Drue, you okay?"

"Yep, fine, just dropped the phone. I didn't realize it wouldn't make it all the way across the kitchen. Who makes a phone cord long enough to reach the door of the fridge, but not inside? I mean, how cruel is that?"

"Drue do you need to put the phone down for a second?"

"Oh." The idea dawned on her. "Yeah, okay, thanks I'll be right back."

The phone went quiet for a few minutes as I heard the clatter of silverware and drawers, of glasses and the ice maker. At last Drue returned. "Okay, I'm set. Now, where were we? Oh yes, why aren't you going to Prom?"

"I don't like dances."

"Totally not good enough."

"I don't have a date."

"Neither do I, but it doesn't mean I'm not going ."

"I just don't want to."

"You get one prom in your life and you aren't going? I dunno Chris."

They were at work, but the guests hadn't arrived yet, so Drue sat on the counter her Diet Coke in hand and swung her legs absently. Bryan brought the silverware and napkins over beside her and began doing roll ups.

"You know you could help."

She looked down at him and made a face. "Yes, I could, but I don't really wanna." She took a sip, "I will though, once I'm done with this." She held the glass in both hands.

He nodded and continued rolling. "So what are your plans for next year?'

"New York."

"Really?"

"Yep, get myself out of this town. What about you? You staying here post graduation?"

He shook his head. "No, definitely not. Hawaii I think."

The words stunned Drue. Her legs stopped swinging and she sat perfectly still processing what was just said. Bryan was leaving. Leaving the city, the state. So are you, Drue told herself. But it was different. Leaving for school meant Drue would be back. There was winter break and next summer. She just assumed she'd come back to find Bryan still there.

"You have a job?" She finally asked.

"Nah, but I'll find something."

"So then why not New York? At least there you'd have a place to crash for a few weeks."

Bryan just shook his head. "Too cold. I would never make it through the winters." He looked up at her, "Are you going to help me with these?"

She looked down at her empty cup. "Oh, right. Sorry." Drue jumped off the counter and picked up some silverware. "I can't believe you are leaving."

"I know it's going to be awesome."

35

May 17th

Scarlette,

They were all there. Chris, his girlfriend, our whole group of friends. But it was as if I only saw him. We were in a boat. Like one of those little rowboats and he was on a platform, slightly raised from the rest of us, the place of honour. The boat moved slowly, there was no rush, none of us were eager to reach our destination.

He was going to war. That was all I knew. He was leaving and this might be the last time I would ever see him. But what did that mean? What did I need to say to him so that I could once and for all have closure? Because there was something, some reason this felt so important. And yet, what could I say with everyone there? I wanted to tell him I was sorry that the friendship thing had never worked out for us, tell him that I loved him, but just in an abstract sense, but mostly I wanted to tell him I was okay, that I was going to be okay, even though I'd always miss him. I wanted to say goodbye, once and for all. And as these thoughts were screaming through my head the boat was slowly approaching the dock. Everyone else was silent and I didn't want to be the first to talk. I didn't want to tell him these things publicly; after all, it wasn't about anyone else. But the thing was, the boat was small, you couldn't walk or move or pull someone aside. There was no saying anything without everyone else listening. So then it became, was it worth telling him I would always care in front of all these people just so he would know? Because I wanted him to know, but I didn't want to make a scene, and I would, because everyone would take it the wrong way. They wouldn't realize I was just saying goodbye. I didn't want anyone else to care. But God I wanted him to know. Still, I remained silent. The boat pulled up to the docks. He got out, waved goodbye. Everyone got out then. He turned left, everyone else turned right. I stood in the middle, just waiting, watching him walk away, and wondering one last time if I should yell after him. But I didn't. I held my tongue, and watched him leave, knowing that I may never get my goodbye.

Then I woke up.

I did go to Prom. So did Drue. Drue took a friend. She liked him, he was a good guy and a good friend but she didn't like him as anything more (which turned out to be a good thing since he later came out as gay) and so there was no romance in the night. It was just a dance. A dance in a beautiful room, full of beautiful people, few of whom meant anything to Drue.

Roger was there. Drue spotted him instantly, sitting in the corner with his girlfriend. Just sitting. Not talking or laughing, not teasing or dancing, just sitting. Drue turned away, she tried to ignore them and when she couldn't anymore she left. She just walked out of the dance hall, not really with any destination in mind, just to leave. Her date didn't notice.

"Drue?"

She was sitting under a ledge of phones, curled up with her knees hugging her chest. I crawled under with her, "Drue you okay?"

She looked at me. Her eyes were dark where the mascara had run. "I put on so much mascara to motivate me not to cry," she said with a sad smile. "It didn't work."

I returned her smile. "What happened?"

"He doesn't look happy." I just waited. "I don't mind that he's with her. Ya know, like yeah it sucks, it sucks that they are something real, that their relationship replaces what him and I were, that now I'm just squashed into the bunch of 'some girl he dated' but beyond that, it's okay, I've moved on. It's just, he doesn't look happy. He's been sitting there, all night. They don't dance, they hardly talk. And I can't even ask him to dance because she'd kill me. I hate that, that I'm not allowed to be his friend. But even that wouldn't matter if I thought he was happy."

I thought of what I could say. Some words to reassure her, but I didn't know if he was happy. And I didn't know if she really wanted to know. We sat in silence.

"You okay?" A group of girls were staring down at us.

Drue nodded. "Yeah, fine, thanks."

When they left, Drue turned back to me, she laughed softly. "What would Prom be without at least one breakdown right?" Then she let out a long breath setting her chin on her knees. "It's just hard, that's all."

"I know."

"Stay." The word surprised her as much as it did him. She had not meant to say it, despite the idea screaming itself through her head all month. Still she had never planned on proposing such a thing. However, now as the word hung between them she couldn't help but wonder if, maybe….

"Drue… I..," it was a stammer, a last attempt to be kind.

Drue gave a small nod, "I know."

He gave her a hug, and a kiss, then turned and walked away. She watched him go knowing that this boy could have been different. But that was also why she knew she would let him go. There would be no phone calls, no tears, and no goodbyes. She didn't want to ruin it, not with this one, she cared too much.

Bryan was her hope for the future. For the first time Drue had fallen for the right kind of boy, not a dream, but reality. And though she realized it too late this time, she knew if it happened once, it could happen again. She might still get her happily-ever-after ending.

So she let him walk out of her life because there was nothing else she could do. She closed her eyes, she could see him smiling at her from across the room, his wide eyes dancing, a private joke she would never know. And as she stood there the summer breeze rustling her hair, a smile crossed her lips for she knew at that moment, that despite all the pain along the way, she would be okay.

36

June 9th

Scarlette,

I graduate next week. Can you believe it? I can't believe that I'm actually done with High School. Feels like I just started. And yet at the same time it feels like an eternity. I mean, God, who was I when I was fourteen? I would hardly recognize that girl now. But at the same time, she's still there, in me somewhere, no matter how buried. After all, I still can't spell, I still can't sit still for long periods of time. So I guess no matter how much you grow up, well you can't lose yourself completely.

All for now, Love always,

A Soon-to-be High School Graduate

"Drue you ready? We don't want to be late!"

"Just a minute!" Drue called back straightening her hat on her head. These awful graduation hats, there was no making them look good. Drue stared at her reflection. This was it, she told her reflection, this was graduation. She cocked her head to one side and then the other staring at the girl looking back at her. Who was that girl? Drue's hair had been straightened for the ceremony, no trace of her ringlets allowed to remain, her face had lost a touch of its roundness accentuating her cheekbones and she wore makeup that make her eyelashes look longer and her lips a slightly darker shade of pink.

She had grown up. The room may be the same as when she moved into it four years before but Drue knew she wasn't that same girl. She had been broken, but she was healing, she had fought and she was winning. She was eighteen years old, an adult. She smiled at her reflection, then wrinkled up her nose and stuck out her tongue, maybe not completely grown up just yet.

"Aw." Drue turned to find Stacey in the doorway, "you look beautiful!" Stacey cooed.

Drue smiled at her sister. "I'm wearing your graduation outfit, but thank you."

Stacey threw her arms around her little sister. "I can't believe you are graduating!"

"I'll take one of those." Drue heard her mother's voice from the doorway. Her mom put her arms around both girls.

Drue heard her parents' door close. "Everyone ready?" Her dad's voice asked as he entered Drue's room. "Hey I don't want to be left out." He scooped all three women into his arms.

"Wow, hey, can't breathe!" Drue called, giggling as her family squashed her. They began to release their grip, but not before Drue was able to catch a glimpse of them in the mirror. All of her family packed together into that tiny room, in that one embrace, as if nothing could ever tear them apart, and maybe, Drue thought, after the last year, nothing could. That or, Drue added with a smile, her family were all just freaks. Either way, Drue had to concede, she was pretty lucky.

Drue went away to college that year. She did something the rest of us couldn't, she got out of California. We stayed in touch, but our lives took us in different directions and so the letters were few and the phone calls fewer. Still, she would tell me about her drunken nights, about the new boys that came and went, about the new friends she was making. And slowly, she grew up. She still fought, sometimes falling, always managing to pick herself up.

That summer she came home. We were already all there.

I had a party. I invited all our old crowd and that meant for the first time in a year, Drue had to see that boy who had changed her so fundamentally that she had once wondered who she was without him. She was scared to see him after so long. Scared it would bring back all the old memories, the pain, and the awkwardness. She didn't want to bring everything back again. But she did it anyway. She came.

He was standing outside with a group of friends talking. He can't remember what about, he forgot it the moment he saw her. She came through the door and began walking toward them. She walked confidently, her head held high as her vision skimmed the scenery around her. It was almost as if she didn't care at all about the group she was walking towards. Her pink heels clicked lightly on the cement and the sun caught her straight auburn hair making it shine. He watched her as she walked toward them and as her gaze came to the group in front of her, she saw him watching her. She smiled and raised her hand in greeting. He raised his hand slightly in replay. "Who's that?" someone asked.

Her heart was pounding. Why did Chris have to send her to usher everyone inside? She opened the door and paused. Of the group, he was one of the few facing her direction. He could see her during the whole walk over. She looked around in embarrassment, was he watching her? Was he judging her? Her knees felt weak, her stomach did a flip and she tried with all her might not to show her nervousness. When she ran out of other things to stare at she at last looked to the group she was approaching. Her gaze went instantly to him. She raised her hand in greeting with a small smile. Was that really dorky, damn what was she doing! She took a deep breath and kept walking the endless ten feet to the group.

"Drue," he answered. He tried to make it sound natural, as if he wasn't shocked by her appearance. He didn't know if he succeeded. How could this possibly be the same Drue he had dated so long ago? She had grown up, but not just grown up, he had grown up. He was taller, perhaps more mature, but otherwise the same. She had grown into herself. She was beautiful, and she knew it. Not in that cocky way a movie star knows it, but in an off handed innocent way as if the knowledge surprised her more than anyone else. She walked up to the group.

"Hey guys," she said, now too scared to look at anyone. "Chris requests your presence inside."

Everyone turned to follow her instructions. He just stood there. It was only for a moment, an extra second, a delayed pause, but she noticed. She smiled. His eyes were wide, his mouth open just slightly. She gave a slight shake of her head, turned on her heel, and ran up to one of her other friends. Roger followed more slowly. With a shake of his head the look of surprise and wonder were gone from his face, the approval washed from his eyes and they did not reappear. But she had noticed, just as I did, from where I stood at the doorway watching the scene play out, and as she passed me going into the house, she winked and I knew that was all she had needed from him. At last she had gotten her goodbye.

I drove her. She didn't invite me in and I didn't offer. We both knew this was something she had to do on her own. So I left her and walked down the street looking in store windows and browsing through the magazines at the check out line. I wondered if she was doing the right thing. She knew I didn't approve, but then she hadn't asked for my approval, she just asked for the ride.

She flipped through magazines on the table. Her heart beat was fast. He called her name and she walked to the back of the room sitting down on the chair he had prepared for her.

"All set?" He asked.

She smiled nervously. "Yep".

"It doesn't hurt that much. Especially not such a small one."

She nodded. "It's all physiological. I freak myself out, but I have a high tolerance for pain."

"That's the case for most people. Let's get started."

She laid back, he took out the needle. "I'm going to start with the small line so you know what to expect for the rest, okay?"

"Okay," her voice was small, far away. She took deep breaths trying to calm herself. She couldn't tell if it was excitement or fear that made her heart pick up tempo, but once it began she knew it was excitement. The anticipation of the feeling that was now playing across her skin, the slight tingling of pain of a perfect, even cut. As her body recognized the sensation, a calmness spread through her.

She felt the artist wipe away the blood that she knew must have appeared and she smiled, letting herself enjoy this feeling for the last time in her life.

"How are you doing?" He asked her.

She didn't open her eyes, just nodded, a half smile resting on her lips. Perfect, she wanted to tell him, she was doing perfectly.

She breathed in and the next cut began. With each cut there existed the simultaneous feeling of wishing the pain to end and wishing it to go on forever. Just as she began to think she could not last a moment longer it was over. She opened her eyes, he was smiling at her.

"All done. You were great."

She smiled back, all the while wanting to cry. It can't be over, it can't be done. What if she was not ready to let it all go?

She walked to the mirror that hung on the back wall of the tattoo parlour. She stared at the small chalice that now sat on her hip. Her symbol for God, for her struggle, for her power, for her success. Most of her scars had disappeared. The ones that did remain on her wrists, her shoulder, and her knee, they would not be there forever, but this one would. No matter what else happened she knew she could not forget this day. This anniversary of her final cut. After all the struggle, depression, attacks and low self esteem she had been clean for a year and knew with some certainty that she'd be okay. No matter what life threw at her, no matter how she struggled, she would be okay, she could make it through.

She walked out of the store. I was there waiting. She smiled at me and I smiled back because I saw in her face something that had not been there in a long time. Calmness. Drue was at peace and I realized that she had finally put it all behind her. She was ready to allow herself to forgive, to move on, and to once again enjoy life. And I realized, with a bit of a shock, that it was a small little chalice that gave her these gifts when no one else could. How ironic, that a cut would be the thing to at last set her free of the self-mutilation of her past. But then, life tends to play itself out over and over again in ironic ways.

It began to rain. Drue gave a shout of laughter opening her arms and twirling in the street.

"Look Chris, it's raining!"

"Yes, yes it is," I replied watching her dance. The tears of the gods, that's what they say right?

Drue turned her face up to the sky and opened her arms in a warm embrace. She knew that somewhere a young girl's heart was breaking and that her world was falling apart. But today, that girl was not Drue, and for now, that was enough.

EPILOGUE

PRESENT DAY: DRUE'S 23RD BIRTHDAY

It is raining outside and I watch the raindrops bounce off the pavement outside as I wait for Drue to finish.

At last she sits staring silently with the last page open in front of her. "Well," I prompt. Then I see the tear in Drue's eyes. "Happy Birthday," I add.

She looks at me and smiles. She closes the manuscript, "It's amazing. Thank you."

"Well, it's by no means perfect. And it's really just a rough draft…"

"No Chris," she pauses, "it's perfect… well, almost."

I raise an eyebrow.

"It's just," she begins, "what about Logan? What about Ciaran?"

"What about them?"

"Well, shouldn't they be in here?"

"Why?" I ask.

She picks up her coffee cup, then puts it back down. She looks around the restaurant: at me, at the counter where two men are talking, at the cashier where a family is checking out the mother with Baby on her hip while Dad runs after the older brother who seems to have disappeared around the bend, then back to me, "It's just...," her eyes slide to the window, a much less intimidating audience than my expectant face, "it was that year that I truly healed. When six months after I got that tattoo and still hadn't cut. When I met Logan who showed me how I deserved to be treated. It was Logan who taught me to dream again and told me I could live those dreams." She presses her hand against the glass leaving an imprint as she takes it away. "He taught me I was worth it. He made me whole."

"He didn't make you whole. You did. That's the whole point Drue." She turns to look at me. I see in her eyes a skepticism that hasn't wavered since she was sixteen years old. "Don't you see," I try to explain. "You did this for yourself. There was no magic in it, no one else fixed you."

She looks at me, then turns back to the window tracing the imprint of her hand, "I dunno." The imprint becomes a bubble version of its original self; she gets annoyed and wipes the area clean. Her eyes turn to me. "I never thought I would be whole again after Roger left. I never thought I would know what it felt like to be that happy. Naïve, I told myself. Your first love you're allowed to be naïve, but then you grow up. You get jaded; you forget what it's like to lose yourself in someone. That's what I thought.

"Then I met Logan. And for the first time someone understood me, understood my dreams and my thoughts, knew what I was trying to say even when I couldn't get the words just right. And I loved him, I truly loved him. So I thought, 'well this is it. This is what a grown up relationship must be like.'"

I wait knowing there is more. Sure enough a moment later she continues, her voice is soft, the inner workings of her mind rather than a monologue dictated to me.

"Months later I met Ciaran. And I lost myself in him. For some reason that is beyond all logic I fell for this boy in a way I believed was only reserved for your first love. But he wasn't my first love; he wasn't even my second love. So don't you see? He showed me I was capable of falling in love again. Like really in love, that kind where the world is a brighter colour, and you can't remember what it must feel like to be sad, and you want to run down the street telling people about this guy that's yours. And who you can watch sleep, or dance, or laugh with his friends, and all are equally enjoyable because he is happy, and that makes you happy. God Chris, there were serenades on the beach, and shooting stars, there were dances in bars and drunken walks homes, there was meeting the friends, and the looks on the girls' faces when they realized I got to go home with the lead singer or the life of the party, I was the girl they took in their arms." She smiles guiltily at me, "I was going to be a roadie for the band, I was going to move to Ireland. That was the year that healed me. It was that year that the world opened its arms to me and took me in and proved to me that your heart breaks, and mends, and breaks again, and if it wasn't for those ups and downs, well then what would be the point of living at all?" She squints up at me, "how can you leave all that out?"

I am silent for a moment, and then I just smile, "Because Drue", I tell her, "that is what the sequel is for."

It is a moment before the words sink in and then Drue breaks into a grin. The tears that have been welling up in her eyes begin to fall and Drue lets out a breath that turns into a laugh. She wipes her eyes. "Alright, fair enough," she says, more from giving in to the argument than realizing that my words are the truth. She smiles sadly at me. "I should go. I have a meeting that I can't be late for." She starts to get up. "It was really nice to see you. Try to come out to New York to visit, ok?"

I stand up and give her a hug, "I'll do my best" I tell her. She turns to leave, "Drue?" She turns back towards me, manuscript in one hand, coat in the other. "It wasn't them that healed you."

She smiles at me, then turns and walks out of the restaurant. I watch my best friend go, waiting. Then it comes. Drue reaches the doorway and turns her face up to the sky. She gives a small skip, a turn in the street. She cannot help it; Drue will always dance in the rain.